Whispering Sea

A Novel

MARIE CAMPBELL

iUniverse, Inc.
New York   Bloomington

Whispering Sea
A Novel

This is a work of fiction. All of the characters, names, incidents, organizations, and dialogue in this novel are either the products of the author's imagination or are used fictitiously.

iUniverse books may be ordered through booksellers or by contacting:

iUniverse
1663 Liberty Drive
Bloomington, IN 47403
www.iuniverse.com
1-800-Authors (1-800-288-4677)

Because of the dynamic nature of the Internet, any Web addresses or links contained in this book may have changed since publication and may no longer be valid. The views expressed in this work are solely those of the author and do not necessarily reflect the views of the publisher, and the publisher hereby disclaims any responsibility for them.

ISBN: 978-1-4502-5382-6 (sc)
ISBN: 978-1-4502-5383-3 (ebk)

Printed in the United States of America

iUniverse rev. date: 09/14/2010

Chapter 1

T he young girl picking up the driftwood stood still. She listened to the fog horn out to sea. It gave her an eerie feeling. Some ship could be in trouble out there.

The mist was getting thicker. She could hardly see the little ramshackle house that was home. The darkness was coming down quickly, ending a miserable November day.

She quickly gathered up the driftwood. It would make a good fire. It was needed. She could feel the chill through the old cloak she was wearing. She hurried to the house. When she entered it was in darkness apart from the dying embers of a fire.

She removed her cloak and nursed the fire back to life. Soon a good blaze lit up the room. A movement in the corner drew her attention. "Father." She scolded the man lying in a makeshift bed. "You very nearly let the fire die and you know how difficult it is to get it started again."

The old man sat up. "Oh my dear I am sorry. I was awake most of last night finishing off this painting." He held it up for the girl to see.

"Oh father it is beautiful. One of the best you have done" It was of a young beautiful woman dancing with a tall fair haired man. Her love for the man was shining from her face as she looked up at him. She was wearing a beautiful yellow dress. Her jet black hair fell in ringlets to her waist. They made a handsome couple, the painting so full of life.

"I think old Marcus will give you a good supply of food for it when you bring it to him and maybe even some candles." Her father sighed. "Oh Serena, dear, dear daughter. Would you mind if I kept this painting? I think it's one of the best I have done or am likely to do. I have been feeling so tired lately."

Serena hugged him. "Of course you must keep it. In the morning we will go through some of your other paintings and I'm sure old Marcus will be delighted to exchange any of them for some supplies."

Serena frowned. She worried about him lately. He slept most of the day. She would ask old Marcus, he was so wise. Maybe he could think of some thing to give him. It seemed to her that they were growing more and more to depend on Marcus's help since they arrived here in Crawford on the Cornish coast.

A sorry pair they must have looked. Her father pushing a hand cart, both soaked to the skin. She was bare footed. Her shoes had long since fallen to bits. They had tried to find shelter in one of the cottage out houses but an angry woman had chased them. There was nowhere for them to go. They had walked miles that day. They were so tired. They had sat down under a hedge and it was there that old Marcus had found them. He took them into his house above his shop, fed them, gave them blankets to wrap themselves in while their clothes dried round his fire.

"Why are you doing this for us?" Father had asked. He had replied. "Because I know what it is like to have nothing. When I arrived here in Crawford many years ago the man who owned this shop befriended me. His wife had died and he seemed to be lonely. He had no family. I stayed with him and helped in the shop. You see, I too was lonely. I never found it easy making friends, real ones. I just got into bad company when my parents died. I just wandered about the country till my footsteps took me here to Crawford. When my friend who owned this shop died, he left it to me and there is an old house on the beach we used as a store. You could stay there for a few days."

Serena smiled to herself. The few days had turned into five years.

She busied herself preparing supper. There was very little food left. She poured water into a saucepan and let it boil on the fire. There was only a handful of meal left on the crock pot. She added this to the boiling water and made a sort of gruel. It would at least warm them and maybe tomorrow they might manage to catch some fish.

When they had eaten she backed up the fire with a slow burning log that would last most of the night. Over the small window she hung a piece of sacking. Not that anyone was likely to look in. Nobody from the village ever came near this part of the beach. There were stories that it was haunted, maybe because there had been a lot of deaths with boats getting washed onto the nearby rocks.

She bolted the door and sat down by the fire looking round the room. There was no need to light the bit of candle that was left. The firelight was bright enough. There was very little in the room. Her father's bed in the corner, an old chest that they used as a table and there were piles of books everywhere.

On a makeshift shelf some plates and tin mugs and by the fire two cooking pots. A string was tied round the mantle piece. This was all they had to dry their clothes. There was no washing tub. All their washing was done in the sea.

Gentle snoring was coming from her father. She kissed him goodnight and made her way up a rickety ladder to a small room beneath the eaves. There was only room for a bed and Serena had rescued two wooden crates from the sea. She used them to keep the little clothes she possessed. Her bed was beneath a small skylight. She loved looking up to the sky before falling asleep. Tonight there were no stars.

She undressed, taking off the outer layers of her clothes and crawled into bed. She thought, as she did every night, how much she loved this house. After all the years of travelling, the roads, the cold and hunger, not knowing where they were going to sleep at night. In no time she was sound asleep.

The sound of someone hammering on the door woke her. She sat up rubbing sleep from her eyes. The room was in darkness. I must have been dreaming she thought. It's the middle of the night. She turned to go back to sleep. The hammering continued. This time she was fully awake.

She made her way down the ladder and crept to the door. Her father's voice behind her whispered. "Go back to bed Serena, I'll answer it." He withdrew the bolt and opened the door a crack but it was pushed wide open and a man almost fell at his feet. "Help me." The man muttered. With the light from the fire they could see that he looked half drowned. A gash on his forehead was pouring blood. "Go and fetch a blanket Serena and I will get him to the fire. He is losing consciousness. I will get his wet clothes off." Her father wrapped him in the blanket and laid him close to the fire. "I wonder what happened to him? To get into such a state. He is very young." Serena bathed his head and bandaged it. She put more wood on the fire. "You go to bed now Serena. I will watch over him."

Serena couldn't sleep. She could hear the man's voice. He seemed to be shouting at someone, giving a warning. It was dawn before there was silence. She crept down to see him. He was asleep.

Chapter 2

Serena woke early. She dressed quickly, anxious to see if the man was alright. She was feeling quite excited. It was a bit of an adventure in her quiet life.

Her father was already up. He had a good fire going. She looked at the man. He looked so different in the morning light. He smiled at her, his bright blue eyes twinkling. He looked quite young, not much older than herself.

"I must thank you both. You saved my life." "Well you were a bit of a drowned rat." Her father said. He smiled. Serena noticed he had perfect teeth. "I am so sorry. I must have frightened you. This is such an isolated place. By the way my name is James Lorrimer. I will never be able to repay you."

"Don't think about that. I am David Church and this is my daughter Serena. I am sorry that we have little to offer you in the way of food. My daughter and I lead very simple lives here. Now Serena, will you go and fetch some water. While you are out James can get dressed."

She wandered slowly along the beach. She was always amazed at the quick changes in the weather. This morning, though cold, it was bright and sunny. The sea, reflecting the blue of the sky, was so calm. It was hard to think that it could be so treacherous.

She filled the bucket at the stream. There was plenty water in it in the Winter months but in the Summer it sometimes dried up and she would have to walk to the other end of the beach for fresh water. She gathered some mint growing at the side of the stream. She could make mint tea for breakfast. She waded into the sea and found some blue mussels. At least their visitor would get something to eat. Later she would go with father to Marcus with one of his paintings.

When she entered the cottage she was amazed at the change in the young man. His clothes though wrinkled were of the best quality. His knee high boots were still drying out by the fire. They too looked as though they had been hand made. It was a miracle that he had managed to swim in them.

He looked up when Serena came in. He continued to stare at her. Serena blushed and felt like running from the room when he said to her. "I think you are the most beautiful girl I have ever met. You look like the girl in the fairy tale Snow White. I think her name was, she had long black hair, beautiful white skin." It was his turn to blush when he said "Her lips like yours, red as a rose." It was too much. Serena took off running like a hare along the beach. I hate him. He was making fun of me. She was remembering one day on her visit to Marcus's shop one of the local girls in buying ribbons for her bonnet sneering at Serena. "Well, well, here's the tinker girl. You won't be buying ribbons for a bonnet. You don't need one with that horse hair you have." Serena had run from the shop in tears. I think I will go back and tell him what I think of him. How dare he make fun of me. Her father came to the door to meet her. "Serena why did you get so upset? The young man was quite genuine in his praise. You must learn to accept compliment when they are given. I for the first time realised that you are no longer a little girl. I have been unfair to you. I think we must soon leave this place. You must find your own way in the world." "Please father don't talk like that. All the years we have been together have been happy ones especially here on the beach. Come now, let's go and have breakfast." James held out his hand when they entered. "I am sorry Serena. Please forgive me but I will defend myself by saying I stand by all I said."

"Now James, you were going to explain your story to us." He sat down by the fire, looking into it's depths, a sad look on his face. "I was an only child. Spoilt, especially by my mother. As a teenager I was constantly getting into trouble. I went to the university but dropped out after a couple of years. I travelled to Africa. Seeing all the terrible poverty there made me look at my own life. How privileged I was and also how terribly selfish. I was determined to get my life sorted out. When I got home I was met by my father. He was grief stricken. My mother had died. He told me that my mother kept asking for me. Father tried tracing me but I had been constantly on the move. He blamed me for mother's death saying that it was worry about me that killed her. I knew that what he said could be partly true and I couldn't take it. So off I went again and it was a few days afterwards that I met two men in an inn. We sat drinking. When they said they had a yacht and would I like to crew with them I jumped at the chance. I was grieving for my mother and angry with my father. I wanted to do anything to ease the hurt and forget.

We were far out at sea when the men informed me that the yacht was stolen. I tried to get them to return but they weren't having it. A thick mist came down very quickly. We sailed too close to a big ship and its wash capsized us. The men escaped in the dingy leaving me to drown. The rest you know."

Dad patted him on the back. "All I can say young man is thank God we were here to help you. Now James, Serena and I are going to the village to get some supplies. We won't be away too long. You rest till we get back."

Marcus watched father and daughter walking towards his shop. He noticed that Serena's father had got very thin and his shoulders quite stooped. He remembered what he had looked like when they first met. Although he was soaked and bedraggled he still had a proud look about him and walked with his head held high.

Serena walking beside him seemed to have changed in a short time from a young child into a lovely young lady. In spite of the strange assortment of clothes she was wearing, most of them from his shop, she was as usual, barefoot. He felt saddened about this. He couldn't persuade her to spend any of the money from the paintings on shoes. He would gladly have given them to her but he knew better than to offer. They had such pride. What use would shoes be to me she had once said. We do all our washing in the sea. I am in and out of it all day. I would have to keep taking them off

David rolled out his painting. "I hope you will be able to sell this one." Marcus looked at it. He was constantly amazed at the beauty of his paintings. He was truly gifted. This one was of a child sitting on a rock, her feet dangling in the sea, a shell held to her ear. He had captured the look of wonder on the child's face.

Marcus looked at the painting. "I like it very much. Have you made a list of the supplies you need? Why don't you go into the back shop. Mrs Bell is there. She has just brought in a pot of tea and cake. She spotted you coming along the road."

Mrs Bell they knew was Marcus' neighbour. She cooked the main meal for him and did a bit of cleaning for him. A few hours work a week. It was a great luxury for them to have real tea and Serena's mouth watered at the thought of cake.

Mrs Bell looked at father and daughter as she poured the tea. Neither she nor anyone else in the village could make head or tail of them. They were well spoken. What on earth had turned them into tinkers and Marcus had told her that one day when they were in the shop and he was in the back he heard them talking fluently in French. David borrowed a lot of books from him. He was Serena's teacher, he told him.

They walked back to the beach house heavily laden. Marcus had given them much more than was on the list. When David had protested Marcus had replied. I will make a very good profit from your painting. Mrs Bell handed Serena a parcel. Some things that were handed in by a woman in the next village. Marcus said they could go in payment along with the groceries.

When they approached the house they noticed the smoke curling up from the chimney. So James had kept the fire going. Serena felt happy. He had not gone, as she feared he might have.

He came to the door to meet them. "I have been busy since you left. Come and see what I have done. They looked about the room and at first they spotted nothing. Then they spotted another bed in the far corner of the room. They were amazed. It was made out of bits and pieces from around the beach. When they said nothing he looked worried. "Have I been too forward? I should have asked first if I could stay for a little while." "Of course you can stay." David and Serena said. "Where did you learn to make something like this?" "When I travelled in Africa I saw the terrible poverty and I was amazed how they managed to make themselves some kind of shelter from next to nothing." "Here about the beach there is an abundance of things. And look I can pay you for letting me stay for a few days." He handed David a leather pouch. There was a jingle of coins. David held it for a moment then he handed it back. "We will take no money from you. You are welcome to share all we have. Now I am very tired. I will lay down for a while. Serena why don't you take James to the next bay. Maybe some wreckage from the yacht could be washed up there."

They wandered along the beach, James stopping now and again to pick up a pretty coloured stone or unusual shell to hand to Serena. They clambered over the rocks, James holding her hand. When she stumbled at one point Serena turned on him angry. "You don't need to hold my hand. I am used to looking after myself and when you go away I will be back to looking after myself." James started to say something then changed his mind. "I think we will have to leave searching till tomorrow. It's beginning to get dark."

When they got home Serena set to preparing supper. It was wonderful having supplies. There was even some candles. She decided to light the bit of old candle. They sat at the makeshift table eating supplies and with the firelight and the candle, the room was transformed.

Serena couldn't remember being so happy. James told them stories about all his wanderings. And he encouraged Serena to talk. She had just started telling him about something that had happened to her and her father when David stood up abruptly and said. "I think that's enough talk for one night. I think we should get ready for bed." Serena felt angry with herself. She should have remembered that her father did not like talking about their life before finding this home on the beach. James was puzzled. Why did David not like Serena talking. He could be so friendly one minute and so stern the next.

Serena did all the usual chores, bade her father and James goodnight and made her way up the ladder to her bed. One of the candles she took with her. She would look in the parcel that Mrs Bell had given her. There was a warm winter cloak, petticoats and skirts. One of the skirts had a matching bodice. It was a bright scarlet colour. Oh it is so beautiful. Would I dare wear something like this. She tried them on. They fitted her perfectly. Why shouldn't I wear them she thought to herself. I wonder if James will like me in them. Then she felt her face growing hot at the thought.

She got up early next morning. Her father and James were still asleep. She put more wood on the fire and tip toed out. She made her way in the semi darkness to the stream for water for the morning tea. She smoothed down the skirt and jacket. Maybe she shouldn't have worn them. They seemed to be too grand for roaming about the beach. She made a decision. She would go home and change before the men woke up but when she went in they were both awake. "Good morning my dear." Her father said. "You are up early this morning." He didn't even notice what she was wearing. But James was different. He was looking at her open mouthed. "You really are a lady." Her father turned to look at her. "You are a bit over dressed my dear." Then he turned to James. "Of course my daughter is a lady. Surely it didn't take fancy clothes for you to see that?"

Once again Serena's father had put him in his place. Serena, seeing his embarrassment, turned to her father. "I think it was very kind of James to say what he did. You didn't even notice what I was wearing.

Anyway I am going up to change." She climbed up to her room, the tears not far off. It was the first time in her life that she had been so cross with the father she thought the world of.

After a time she came back down. Her father immediately apologised and gave her a hug. "I am just becoming a bad tempered old man. James has gone out walking along the beach. Do go and bring him back for breakfast."

Serena found him staring out to sea. "Do come back in James. I am so worried about my father. I have never known him to get so cross. I was going to have a word with Marcus but the opportunity never came." James turned to her. "Don't worry about me Serena. I'll tell you what. I will have to go to the village to buy some clothes. You and your father have kindly let me stay a while." "Why don't you come with me and you can talk to Marcus. Your father might be happy to have the place to himself. He told me he is planning to paint another picture." "Oh what a great idea James. And I could wear the scarlet clothes." She is still just a little girl James thought to himself.

Serena hurried with her chores and her father waved them off. James was right. He seemed to be happy left alone. When they entered the village a lot of sweeping of doorsteps took place. James laughed. "We are creating a lot of attention." Which indeed they were.

Serena took him to the small drapers shop. "I will leave you here while I go to talk to Marcus. When you are finished you can collect me there."

Marcus was delighted to see her and Mrs Bell, hurrying in, clasped her hands together in excitement. "I knew. I just knew that you would look beautiful in these clothes. Will I make a pot of tea Marcus?" "Maybe later Mrs Bell. I think that Serena would like to talk to me first." Wise old Marcus Serena thought. They sat down in a corner of the shop and Serena told him about the worries she had about her father.

"He seems so different Marcus. He is getting quite short tempered and he seems to want to sleep all the time. Can you give me something to help him?"

Marcus sat for a while in silence then he held Serena's hand. "I don't think that I or a doctor can help your father. All the years that you have been wandering, getting soaked and not eating properly has taken it's toll on his body. I have noticed such a change in him the last four months. I think there is something on his mind as well. Will you tell him to come and visit me. I would like to have a talk with him." "I think I know what you are trying to tell me Marcus." Said Serena, tears streaming down her cheeks. "No Serena." Marcus said. "It is not my place to tell you anything. What you have to hear must come from your father. Go now Serena. Tell your father that there is something important I want to talk to him about. Go and find the young man. I don't think you will want to sit having tea."

She met James out on the road. He was carrying a parcel with his new clothes. He looked so happy until he saw Serena's tear stained face. "What on earth is the matter Serena? Come, let's walk home." I'll talk to you when we leave the village." Serena whispered through her tears.

Chapter 3

T hey walked in silence then, sitting down on the rocks near the shore, Serena told him what Marcus had said. "But Serena that doesn't mean that your father is going to die or anything." This brought another flood of tears. "James I'm afraid that it means exactly that. I have watched my father going downhill for a long time. You should have known him even a year ago. I wasn't wanting to admit the change in him, hoping that Marcus would have a cure. James held her close until her sobbing ceased..

"Has it always been just you and your father?" He asked. "I don't remember my mother but sometimes I think I do. I keep getting a picture in the mind but it is so fleeting. There was a sound of music and people were dancing. I was sitting on a stair watching. I must have done something wrong because a women was pulling at me saying naughty child. Then a beautiful women in a yellow dress lifted me up and twirled me round. She was laughing and I was so happy. Then there was the noise of shouting and screaming and I was sitting on a horse, my father holding me in front of him galloping away from the noise.

The yellow dress the woman was wearing was just like the one that father had painted. So you see James maybe father had done another painting of a women in a yellow dress and I had memories of it. And if it wasn't good enough father would have destroyed it which he done quite often if unhappy with it. That is why his recent one he is so proud of and wont sell it to Marcus. So you see James how mixed up everything is in my mind and father would never discuss my mother so I never asked because it made him unhappy."

"So how old were you when you rode off with your father?" Serena thought for a moment. "I think about three. I remember feeling so tired. I think we rode for miles and miles."

They sat for a while in silence, each with their own thoughts, James realising, not for the first time, the wonderful childhood he had had and how selfish he had been to cause his parents such unhappiness. And here was Serena, in his eyes still a child, accepting such hardships.

He turned to her. "You have had a hard life." She smiled at him. "Not at all James. I have had the most wonderful life travelling the country with my father. Oh I know that there have been times when I have been cold and hungry but then something lovely would happen and we would forget these awful days. After about a few months father had to sell the horse. He found an old pram to carry our few possessions and sometimes when I got tired I would ride in it. I remember one time father left me in the pram while he went into a shop. I was curled up in it, my head squashed against the hood. A nosy old women peering in to look at the baby got the shock of her life at the monster lying there. And when father came out of the shop she went to hit him. A disgrace keeping a girl that age in a pram. Another time we were passing a field when father pointed. Look Serena at that scarecrow. The jacket it's wearing is better than the one I am wearing. I'm going to get it. He climbed over the fence and was trying the scarecrow's jacket on when we heard loud laughter. It was a cheery red cheeked woman. Well I never. Now I have seen everything. She went into another fit of laughter. My father, so embarrassed, tried to be dignified. I am very sorry madam he said to her. The woman stopped laughing. Look here would you like some work. I am the farmer's wife and we are in the middle of harvesting the fruit. We can always do with extra help.

And so it was. We stayed there for the whole of the summer. We stayed in out houses. There was a big crowd of pickers. Father wasn't very good at picking to begin with. In fact I could fill the baskets just as quick as him with my small fingers. At night one of the pickers played a violin and there would be singing and dancing. It was such a happy time. There were lots of children there. When the picking season ended they all had homes to go back to. They nearly all came from the city and once a year they would be off to the country. It was like a holiday to them."

Here Serena looked sad. "The last harvest for picking was potatoes and after that sadly we had to go back on the road. When we left the white frost was on the ground but with the money that father had made we had good boots and warm clothes."

Serena jumped to her feet. "Oh James I have been doing such a lot of talking. You must be bored listening to me. Look the sun is going down." As indeed it was, sinking into the sea in a final burst of orange and gold. "Father will be worried. We must hurry home." She held out her hand. "Thank you James for listening to me."

"Tell me Serena, what happened to you after the farm? I really would love to hear your story."

"Some other time James. Now please do hurry."

"So here you are. I was beginning to think that I would have to go looking for you."

"Sorry father." Serena gave him a hug. "I have been talking to James about some of the things that happened to us while we were wandering the roads."

Her father looked angry. He glared at James. "I don't think it's any of your business James and I don't think Serena should satisfy your curiosity about our lives." He turned his back on them and busied himself putting more wood on the fire.

Serena and James looked at each other but said nothing and after a while he was his usual good natured self When Serena told him that Marcus was wanting to talk to him he seemed to be delighted. "I will go tomorrow."

But that night one of the worst storms for many years hit the coast.

It was the sound of the wind that woke Serena. It came as such a surprise after such a beautiful night. It had been so calm with such a glorious sunset. As she lay the wind got stronger and stronger and was howling round the house with a noise like a banshee.

She dressed hurriedly and scrambled down the ladder. James and her father were up sitting by the fire.

"This is a bad one Serena but this is a strong little house." No sooner had he spoken when there was the sound of something crashing on the roof. "I think that's your chimney gone." James said. "I'll go up and see if there is damage in your room Serena." After a minute he shouted down. "I'll have to shift your bed. The skylight has been blown in. Your bed is getting soaked."

The storm continued through the night. At one point hail stones came down the chimney, almost putting the fire out. They sat all night round the fire, huddled in their blankets.

When the dawn came the wind dropped. They could hear the crashing of the waves on the rocks but apart from that it was as if there had been no storm. Everything was so calm.

After a while they ventured out to inspect the damage to the house. Part of the chimney had collapsed as well as the skylight.

Serena dried her bedclothes round the fire. Her father and James walked along the beach to see if they could find something to mend the skylight. They found a large piece of canvas. It looked as if it had come from a sail. James said nothing but thought to himself it could have come from the stolen yacht.

"This will be excellent to mend the skylight. I will do it when we get back though I don't think it will last another storm."

"Maybe you should give up living here David and maybe find something in the village."

"I think that maybe you are right James. Maybe you are right."

James looked at him. It was as if his thoughts were far away.

When they went back to the house Serena had cooked breakfast. Porridge and some pancakes with the precious flour and eggs that had been given in the supplies. David smiled at Serena. "Well my dear you have been extravagant." "Well father let's just say we are celebrating being alive."

Once again James thought where did this young girl get all her courage.

"I am going to see Marcus today." David announced. "Will you manage to fix the skylight on your own James?" "Of course I will manage David." "You have been a great help to us James. It was blessing that brought you to our door."

It was late afternoon when David returned. He seemed to have changed. There was a happy air about him. Serena and James looked at each other. What had old Marcus said to him to make him so changed. When Serena asked him all he would say was a heavy load had been lifted from my shoulders.

Serena was out wading at the edge of the sea when James approached. "Look James." She held up a bucket. It was full to the brim with all sorts of shell food.

"We will have a real feast tonight. The storm has washed them in."

"Aren't you cold standing there? Come on Serena let's walk to the other end of the beach." "No James. I'll race you there." And she was off, her long black hair flying behind her. She had tucked her dress up above her knees when she was wading in the sea. She was so natural. She really looked as if she belonged and was part of the sea and all the nature around.

I don't think I will ever forget this picture of her he thought. They sat on a rock to get their breath back.

"Listen James. Do you hear anything?" He listened for a moment. "No I hear nothing." "Listen again. It's the sound from the sea. Don't you hear it whispering?"

James listened again and sure enough the sea was making a whispering sound.

"Gosh Serena. What a wonderful thing to think of. A whispering sea."

They sat in silence for a while. "You were going to tell me what happened to you after you left the farm."

"I told you that when we left the farm the frost was on the ground. We walked for miles. It was beginning to get dark. There was no shelter. I think that maybe for the first time I was close to tears. I think I was missing the farm. We rounded a bend in the road and down below us there was a wood and a light flickering in the trees. Our spirits soared. Where there was a wood there was shelter.

As we approached we realised that the light we had seen was from a fire in a large clearing. It was a gypsy camp. As we approached two or three dogs came running towards us, barking and snarling. One big one seemed to be the leader. I bent down and clapped it. Immediately it stopped snarling and licked my hand. The others backed away. Well I'm blowed. A man's voice said. I have never seen anything like it. Old rusty here would have had the hand of a stranger who touched him. He is our best guard dog.

He led us into the camp and when an old man and woman came out of their caravan to see what all the noise was about the man told them how I had patted old Rusty. Well well. The old woman said. I think they deserve some food and shelter for the night.

From that night they showed us nothing but kindness. The old man and woman seemed to be the ones the others listened to. We found out later that they were nearly all related to each other.

After a few days I went with one of the women into the village. We went from door to door selling things from her basket. She told me to smile. A smiling face helped to sell she said. After a while I was given my own basket and soon I was selling more than she was.

Father too was happy. He was taught all sorts of things. How to make baskets and how to set snares for rabbits. At night we would all sit round the fire. Sometimes the women would sing. Maybe only beating time by knocking two stones together. I will never forget this way of life, so simple and happy. I am not forgetting the hard times when nobody wanted to buy from the baskets, when the men couldn't find odd jobs and when a storm nearly destroyed some of the caravans.

One day we saw two horsemen approaching. The old man told father and I to stay in the caravan. Not to come out till they left." The dogs were growling round the two men. They didn't come down from the horses. I heard them saying. Have you seen a man and child. We were told that they were seen in this area. The old man shook his head. Well it's very important that they are found. We have been searching the country far and wide. There is a reward.

The dogs were getting more and more ferocious, snapping at the horses legs. The old man never called them off. The two men gave up and galloped away.

When we came out from hiding the gypsies gathered round us. I couldn't understand what was happening and I still don't know.

Father and the old man sat by the fire talking and later father told me that we would be leaving. I knew that it had something to do with the two men on horseback. When I asked father he just said don't worry about it. We must start packing. Father, with the help of the men, had made a hand cart. They had made it out of two wheels found at a rubbish dump and bits and pieces of wood scrounged here and there. We packed all our bits and pieces in it and the old woman brought out a basket of food. To last you a few days on your journey she said. There were tears in her eyes and I think my father and I were close to tears leaving such good friends."

Chapter 4

J ames tossed and turned in his makeshift bed. How could Serena's father be so selfish to bring up his daughter in such hardship? It was obvious that he himself had had a good education, even travelling abroad to further his painting. Oh yes he had taught Serena well. He had to admit that. But it was obvious to him that he was running away from something. Who were the two men who had turned up at the gypsy camp looking for them?

It was early dawn before he slept but in the night he had made his decision. It was time he left. He was becoming caught up in their lives. Not only that, he felt a need to see his father, to make up to him for all the kindness he had received from him all his life but had shown him and his mother utter selfishness.

In the morning he walked along the beach with Serena. Neither of them spoke.

"Come and sit for a minute Serena. I want to talk to you." She looked at him. "You are leaving James aren't you?" He put his arm round her shoulder. "Yes it's time I went. I am going back to my father." He bent to kiss her cheek. She turned her head and he found himself kissing her on the lips. They felt so soft, like the petal of a flower. He drew back. "Oh Serena I am so sorry." She put her hand over his mouth. "Please don't say that. Come now. Let's tell father that you are leaving. He will be upset. He has grown quite fond of you."

They made their way back to the house. Serena felt such happiness at the kiss. She put her hand to her mouth. She could still feel the gentleness of his lips and then there was such sadness at the thought of him leaving.

That same day he left. "I'll come back to see you one day." She walked with him to the end of the beach then she held out her hand. "Good bye James." Then she turned and ran back to the house, the tears blinding her.

Her father met her at the door. "I will miss James. He was good company. But come Serena I want to talk to you. It's quite important. The other day when Marcus and I had a talk he suggested that we move into his house. He has two small rooms that have only been used as junk rooms. He suggested that maybe you and Mrs Bell could get them sorted out. And maybe if you agreed you could help him out in the shop as payment for them."

Serena looked at her father. He was pale faced and anxious looking, waiting for her reaction.

"Oh father what a splendid idea. I was getting worried about this house. I don't think the roof will last another storm." And to herself she thought. Clever old Marcus to put it to her father in such a way that it saved his pride.

Serena hugged him. "Now father . There are only two days till Christmas. Can we please have it here on the beach. We have had such lovely Christmases here." And so it was decided. Serena had so many things to think about that the hurt of James leaving was pushed to the back of her mind. She set to making the simple arrangements for the last Christmas in a place that they had had such happy times in. While her father slept she took her fishing rod and went out to the rocks. Maybe she would be lucky. A fish would be nice for Christmas Day. In no time she caught three. The storm must have brought them close to the shore. Because they would be leaving the day after Christmas they could make a feast of all the supplies that were left.

Christmas Eve they lit a huge fire on the beach. It was a beautiful night. The sky looked like black velvet with the stars shining like diamonds. At midnight they heard the church bells from the village

This night I will remember forever Serena thought as they wished each other a happy Christmas.

In the morning they exchanged their presents. Serena had bought her father some brushes for his painting. They weren't new but of quite good quality. She had found them among all the bric a brac in Marcus's shop.

Her father gave her a rolled up painting tied with ribbons. It was a picture of a beautiful house. It looked like some of the pictures she had seen of the colonial mansion houses with it's huge pillars and veranda. The garden sloped in terraces down to a huge pool with fountains spraying on to the pink and white water lilies. It looked so real. Two or three figures were walking in a rose garden.

"Father it is so beautiful and so real with all the little details you have painted in it. Have you seen this house somewhere father? And oh. You have even given it a name. Shannon House." Her father smiled. "Maybe Serena. Maybe in the mists of time I have."

Serena busied herself preparing the Christmas meal. It gave her no pleasure that for once in her life she had plenty food to cook.

Her father, busy rolling up the remainder of his pictures and some of his little bits and pieces, stood for a minute looking round the little house that had given them shelter. Serena, coming in from building up the fire on the beach, saw a look of pure misery on his face. She tip toed quietly back outside.

The next morning they walked the length of the beach, not speaking, each busy with their own thoughts. They climbed over the rocks towards the village and soon the house and beach was lost to view.

Marcus stood at the door of his shop to welcome them. And Mrs Bell had prepared tea in the back room. She bustled about chatting away all the time. "We will get on just fine Serena and maybe you will rest here David while Serena and I get started cleaning out the room. I have already started on it." She turned to Marcus standing by the door.

"Such a lot of rubbish you were holding on to."

"Well my dear Mrs Bell some of the rubbish you were wanting to get rid of has come in handy. The old stove for instance and the old chest full of pots and pans."

Mrs Bell smiled. "As usual Marcus you are right. All these things need is a good clean."

Mrs Bell showed Serena the two rooms. She clapped her hands. "Oh Mrs Bell it will be like living in a palace." The rooms were small but they each had a window looking down on to the road and in the distance the cliffs and the sea. They worked all day cleaning and scrubbing. Between the rooms was a large landing and Mrs Bell suggested that it could be used as a kitchen with the cooking stove and part of an old dresser to keep their pots and pans. "Marcus the kind soul that he is likes his bit of privacy and this way you won't have to share his kitchen."

In no time the rooms were spick and span. Most of the furniture had been covered up good solid oak now shining with the lavender smelling polish.

Mrs Bell appeared from her own house with a pile of bed clothes. "These things I never use. I am just as bad as Marcus for hoarding things." When they finished they joined Marcus and Serena's father for supper. Then it was time for them to climb the stairs to their new home. David shook Marcus's hand but Serena, full of joy, threw her arms round Marcus and hugged him. He blushed with embarrassment and pleasure. To cover up he growled at her. "Maybe tomorrow you will think differently when you come to help me in the shop. I can be quite bad tempered."

In no time Serena got used to working in the shop. In fact it did not seem like work. She loved raking about finding old lovely bits and pieces that Marcus had collected over the years. For the first few days it seemed that the whole village visited the shop curious to see the girl from the beach working there. Her father was quite content to stay in his room. Most of the time he slept. Marcus was quite content to sit in a corner with his beloved books.

Soon Serena got to know the villagers. They were mostly shy but like everywhere there was always one or two spiteful. One woman in particular only came into the shop to say something nasty to her. She would go round picking up things and putting them back, never buying anything. "This must be a change for you." She said one day. "Not going around begging. Marcus better watch out. Things could start disappearing." When Serena told Mrs Bell she patted her on the shoulder. "Don't let her get to you. That will be Isa Jones, a bitter woman. She is always causing trouble. She has collected a few cronies round her."

The weeks passed. Serena so happy that she stopped worrying about her father's health. So it came as a shock to hear him moaning in the middle of the night. Marcus too was awakened. He took one look at David and said. "I am going for the doctor. I'll shout Mrs Bell to come in to stay with you." Serena bent over her father. The moaning had stopped. He opened his eyes and tried to speak but only a whisper came out. "I love you Serena. I am so sorry." She bent closer. "I have left it too late to tell you." Then he whispered "Shannon." The doctor came in and bent over him. "I am sorry Serena. Your father has gone."

Serena felt numb. She couldn't even cry, her sense of loss was so terrible. Her father had been with her every day every hour of her life from the age of three. He had been her teacher and her friend.

Marcus and Mrs Bell were a tower of strength. They made all the funeral arrangements and he was laid to rest near the house on the beach. One of the spots he had loved. After the funeral Serena went and sat on the rocks. It gave her comfort to listen to the whispering sea gently flowing on to the beach.

Serena threw herself into working in the shop. Marcus had surrounded himself with loads of clutter. One part of the shop was a sort of pawn shop. The other half sold the villagers basic needs, flower, meat, vegetables etc. bought from the local farmers. Crawford was a fishing village. When the fishing was poor the villagers knew hardship and this was when the pawn side of the shop was a god send to them.

Serena soon got to know everyone. They treated her with suspicion to begin with, then for the most part she liked them, except for Isa Jones who was determined to make life difficult for her.

It was some weeks after her father's death. She was busy sorting out some of the clothes, putting them on hangers. Most of them were good quality, sent into the shop by well off people. Many a poor family were grateful for them including herself, remembering how happy she had been with the scarlet skirt and bodice.

A voice interrupted her. "Is there anyone serving in this shop?" It was Isa Jones. Serena came out from behind all the clothes. "I am sorry Mrs Jones. I didn't hear you come in." Isa Jones was standing with her arms full of what Serena thought was rags. "How much will you give me for this lot?" Serena looked round for Marcus's help but he must have fallen asleep after his lunch and she didn't want to waken him.

"I'm sorry Mrs Jones but I am afraid that I can't give you anything. They are not suitable for selling." Isa Jones pushed her face right up to Serena. "What do you mean you can't give me money." Serena felt like saying because they are dirty and smelling but instead she just stuck to her guns and refused to give her money. For a minute she thought that she would strike her but she just gave her a look of pure hatred and marched out of the shop.

When she told Marcus what had happened he looked worried. "You have made an enemy there. She thought you were an easy target to get money. She was probably watching the shop to make sure you were alone. She knew better to try something like that on me because I would have barred her from the shop."

Later that afternoon Marcus persuaded her to have a walk round the village. "You have been inside too long. A walk will do you good but you better wrap up well. There is still snow on the ground and it's starting to freeze."

Serena set off really enjoying her walk. She hadn't realised how much she missed being outside. She walked further than she intended. It was beginning to get dark. When she turned the corner near the shop she saw a crowd of children. They were throwing snowballs at each other.

As she passed one hit her at the side of her head. It felt more like a stone. She turned. It wasn't a young child it was a boy of about fourteen who threw it and this was confirmed when he shouted. "Come on pelt her." The snowballs were rained on her from all directions. Eventually she stumbled and fell to the ground. "Serves you right you bitch." The big boy shouted. "That will teach you. So you couldn't give my mother money for the clothes." He swore again and went to kick her. A man's voice stopped him. "You young ruffian. You and your gang clear off before I get the law on you." They ran off but the big boy, still defiant, shook his fist at them. "I'll sort her out yet." He shouted.

The man helped her to her feet. "Come, I'll take you to your home. He saw Serena, badly shaken, was grateful for the support of his arm. Marcus was alarmed when he saw the state Serena was in. The man explained what had happened. He helped Marcus to get her seated by the fire and while Marcus made her a hot drink he bathed the cut at the side of her head.

After a while the dazed feeling left her and she turned to thank her rescuer. He was a very handsome man she thought. Dark hair and dark eyes, almost black coloured. His accent wasn't from around the area. He was younger than she first thought.

Marcus invited him to stay for supper but he said he had to go. He had some business to attend to in the area. He shook hands and once again Marcus and Serena thanked him. "I think they would have killed me if you hadn't come along. They were like a pack of wolves."

The next morning she insisted in helping in the shop but she kept looking out in case Isa and her son appeared. But there was no sign of them. "No." Mrs Bell said. "They have been sending some of the younger children in to the shop. There are about six of them. The father ran off and left them as soon as the older ones could earn money." They are a strange family. The father owned a small fishing boat. When he married Isa the locals shook their heads. Apparently she was from a rough family, always getting into trouble for stealing and poaching. When the two eldest boys grew up they seemed to take over their father's boat. They treated him badly till one day he just left. I believe he now lives in Darwood, the next town. A strange thing about the Jones family. There are times when money seems plentiful. Then they all troop off to the town, come back laden with packages and the drunken parties go on for days. Then as you have seen, they have nothing. The little ones especially I feel sorry for. That lump of a boy that attacked you should be working. Plenty of things he could be doing to help his family."

A few days later her rescuer appeared at the shop. "I just stopped by to see if you are alright. I don't think I even introduced myself properly. I am Owen Gray." He held out his hand. "I am Serena and this is my friend Marcus who owns this shop." "And what are you doing in this area? We don't often see visitors here." Marcus asked him.

"Well I am just recovering from an illness. I do a bit of painting and a bit of fishing. I like the quietness. I have a small boat. It's anchored in one of the quiet coves."

Chapter 5

H e turned to Serena. Maybe one day you would show me around. I believe there are some interesting caves around this area. "I would be delighted to show you around. Why don't you stay and have lunch with us. Marcus could tell you some of the history of the village." "Yes of course I will. Marcus said but he was frowning."

Serena was happy. Not since James left had she had a companion to go walking with. Ever since the Jones family attacked her she had been afraid to go for walks on her own.

One day she spoke to Marcus about her father's room that had been empty since his death. "Do you think it would be a good idea to rent it out to Owen? It would be better for him than living on his boat."

Marcus had turned to her, a frown on his face. "No Serena. I don't think it would be a good idea. We hardly know him and don't you think that you are seeing a little too much of him."

Serena was taken aback. It was so unlike Marcus and after all hadn't he taken her and her father in not knowing anything about them. So the matter was dropped but she still walked with Owen most afternoons when she finished all her chores.

She had more or less taken over the shop. As the months went by everything was now neat and tidy. Marcus didn't mind as long as she kept away from his precious books.

She was a bit puzzled by Owen. He never talked about himself and once when she suggested that maybe they could go fishing in his boat he said that the cove was too far away where it was anchored. He seemed to be content exploring the coves and caves near the village. Once when she stumbled on the rocks he put his arms round her but let her go quickly. Serena, remembering James' hug so full of warmth and affection, was puzzled at his coldness.

Something else she was finding strange was his growing friendship with the Jones family. Once or twice she spotted him coming from their house. The eldest girl was quite pretty though her tongue was as wicked as her mother's. Surely he didn't fancy her? When she mentioned this to Marcus he looked at her for a moment. "One can never tell about these things. What attraction there can be between a man and woman. Remember Mr Jones. At one time he must have found Isa attractive enough to marry her against all advice."

Marcus looked worried. "Please Don't think I'm being forward Serena but tell me. Do you have feelings for Owen?" Serena hugged him. "Oh Marcus. Of course not. I really enjoy walking with him and of course I am grateful to him for rescuing me from the gang of louts." I find him just a bit cold and maybe even a bit self centred."

Marcus patted her hand. "I am glad Serena. You know that you are like a daughter to me. Your life, though hard, has been sheltered from the outside world and you are so young."

Mrs Bell appeared in the shop her arms full of mops and dusters. "I thought since it's such a lovely spring morning that we might do some cleaning."

Marcus growled. "It's the same every year." He turned to Serena. "I get no peace. The way she goes on you would think we lived in a pig sty."

"Now now Marcus. You won't be shifted around. Serena has already done the shop so you can sit there in peace." He grumbled his way through to the shop. Mrs Bell and Serena smiled at each other. They knew that he would be quite happy sitting there with his books and attending to the odd customer.

In no time it was late afternoon. The house from top to bottom was scrubbed and polished. Mrs Bell turned to Serena. "You know Serena there is another room we haven't cleaned. I know you haven't been near your father's but now I think it's time. I will leave you to do it yourself in private."

Mrs Bell was right. She hadn't been near the room. She found it too painful remembering her father struggling to talk to her. What had he wanted to say and why after the years they had spent alone together had he not talked about his past that she so desperately wanted to hear.

She made her way into his room. Nothing had been touched apart from all the bedding Mrs Bell had removed. She lay on the bare mattress and a storm of tears shook her body. She cried for her father but she also cried for herself. What would have become of her if old Marcus had not given them a home? Would her father have died in some roadside ditch, leaving her to face the world alone? She dried her tears and for the first time felt anger at her father.

She looked around the room. In the chest of drawers his brush and comb and some toilet things. A few odd bits of clothing lay on a chair. In a corner two of his paintings that he wouldn't part with and some of his precious paints and brushes. She looked at the paintings. The one with the lady in the yellow dress seemed to leap out at her. It really was a wonderful painting. The other painting of a beautiful house that her father had called Shannon. Why were they so special to him? Even when he was dying his last words as she lent over him had been Shannon. She felt an emptiness inside. He could have told her so much. He had deprived her of a past.

The next day she felt calmer. She was happy working in the shop. She decided to rearrange the shop window and as a centrepiece she put the picture of the lady in the yellow dress.

Nearly all the village came to look in the window, the older women with a touch of sadness, knowing that their time of wearing something so beautiful had passed. And the young girls hoping that maybe, just maybe, they would dance with such a handsome man and wear such a beautiful dress.

The shop was never so busy. It took her and Marcus all their time to serve them all. Curiosity about the picture drew them in but they stayed to buy. At the end of the day Marcus handed Serena a little velvet draw string bag. "I have put ten gold sovereigns in there. Some day you will leave this shop and village. You have become like a daughter to me and when you leave to go into the world it will give me comfort to know that you won't be destitute."

Serena tried to refuse the money. "But Marcus I am happy here with you. I don't ever
want to leave."

Marcus smiled. "You are so young Serena. You are just like a fledgling bird gull happy in a warm nest. But then one day it wants to try out its wings and it flies away from the nest just as you will some day.

Serena, hanging out the washing, felt the heat of the sun. It was such a beautiful day. The cold winter days had passed. She looked down at the sea. Today it was so calm and the blueness of the sky was reflected in it. I will go for a walk down there when I finish my chores. I don't think the Jones family will bother me. Owen has frightened them off. Then she realised that she hadn't seen Owen for some time. Oh well she thought to herself. I suppose he has better things to do than to accompany someone young on her walks. But she still couldn't understand how he could have become so friendly with the awful Jones family.

It was early evening when Serena returned from her walk. It promised to be a beautiful night. The full moon had already started to rise.

When she went in the lovely smell of baking met her. Mrs Bell was in the kitchen.

"I just popped in with a steak pie. It's in the oven keeping warm. We were beginning to worry about you." Serena felt a tightness in her chest. She turned away so they wouldn't see her tears. These two dear friends who made her feel so safe and loved.

Chapter 6

Serena awoke. It seemed as though she had just fallen asleep. Someone was shouting her name. At first she thought she was dreaming. Her room was bathed in moonlight. The shouting continued then she recognised Marcus's voice. He was standing at the bottom of the stairs.

"Something is going on in the street. The whole village seems to be awake. There is a lot of yelling and swearing and it's one o'clock in the morning." Then Marcus looking through the window gasped. "Good heavens it's the prison wagon."

Serena looked. A long black wagon with iron bars was stopped outside the Jones' house. The shouting and yelling was disturbing the two horses pulling it. A lot of strange men were racing from house to house pulling the local men from their beds and throwing them into the big black wagon and among them struggling and swearing were the men from the Jones family.

Then it was Serena's turn to gasp. Believing himself to be hidden in the shadows was Owen. He was mounted on a black horse that blended in with the shadows. He would maybe not have been discovered if the moon that had been hidden in the clouds had not burst forth, bathing him in it's full light.

The black wagon moved off. The whole village it seemed, trying to stop it's progress. When it disappeared the crowd still milling about, undecided what to do. Then someone spotted Owen. A cry went up. They converged on him. Let's get him. The spy for the Excise. Owen dug the spurs into the horse and he almost flew down the road.

Serena looked at Marcus. She was pale with shock. "Do you think it's true. Was Owen really a spy?"

"I'm afraid it's true. Nobody in the village would have betrayed them and from what I could see they knew exactly the houses to raid."

"But Marcus does that mean that when he walked with me along the beach and was prowling about the caves that he was using me as a cover up?"

Marcus, about to reply, noticed that the crowd, getting more loud and angry was starting to converge on the shop. The yell went up. Where's the tinker girl? She was helping him out, spying with him along the beach.

"Quick Serena go upstairs. This crowd is ugly." Thank goodness for the window shutters as the stones battered the front of the shop.

Then someone suggested that they get a ladder on to the roof and get in one of the skylights. They were like hounds out for the kill.

Serena was terrified. Marcus held her hand. "Now Serena listen to me. That mob won't be happy till they get to you. They have got to have someone to blame. Some of the men taken away will maybe never see their families again. The county is up in arms against the smugglers especially since England and France are at war. And France making money selling to the smugglers though of course most of the smuggled goods end up on the rich man's table."

They heard the clatter of the ladder and the yells of the crowd encouraging the men to get on the roof.

Suddenly above the noise was the sound of a bell and a woman's voice. It silenced the crowd. It was Mrs Bell standing bravely in front of the crowd.

"You all ought to be ashamed. Wanting to harm a young girl, an innocent girl. She didn't know that Owen was spying."

There were some in the crowd still growling. Mrs Bell silenced them with her next words. "I know each and every one of you and if you don't all go to your homes I will report you to the Magistrate and you will all lose your homes." One by one, still angry, they moved to their homes.

Marcus opened the door to let Mrs Bell in. "You are a wonderful brave woman."

She laughed. "Well what did you think of the bell. Didn't you recognise it? It's the one from above the shop door. I took it home to clean it."

Then she turned to Serena. "My poor child. It didn't matter what I said. These people get an idea into their heads and they won't let it go. They will still want to do you harm. You will have to leave the village for your own safety and I think you must go at once before they all gather together again."

Marcus, the tears in his eyes, agreed. "Go now my dear and pack your things. Make for Dorward but try to keep off the main road. There could be village people travelling there to work."

Serena quickly packed her few possessions. She looked round the room, the only home she had ever really had. Mrs Bell and Marcus dear dear friends she would maybe never see again. Mrs Bell was shouting up the stairs.

Chapter 7

"Do hurry Serena. The crowd are beginning to gather again. Their mood is ugly. They are determined for vengeance."

Mrs Bell quietly opened one of the windows at the side of the house away from the street. One last tearful farewell and she clamoured out into an overgrown garden. Nettles and blackberry bushes scratched and stung her. Thankfully the moon had disappeared behind a cloud and she was some distance from the village before it reappeared to guide her. Keeping well away from the road she ran and stumbled for miles and when daybreak came she found shelter in a wood and lay completely exhausted. She slept and the morning was well advanced when she awoke. Her feet, arms and legs were covered in scratches. She bathed them in a nearby stream. They stung. She felt so lonely. The tears streamed down her cheeks. She thought, why has all this happened to me? Then, being young, she pulled herself together. She tidied her hair and brushed down her clothes. Heaving the bag onto her back she started walking. Surely she wasn't too far from Dorward a bigger town. She could maybe get work there and it was far enough away from Crawford. But she would have to be careful. Marcus did say that some of the Crawford villagers worked there.

It was late afternoon when she limped into Dorward. Nobody paid much attention to her.

Lots of people were on the road. These days there was little work. She decided to walk through the town nearer to the outskirts. There would be less chance of meeting anyone from Crawford there.

She started to feel so tired. Lack of food was taking its toll. She came on a coaching inn just when she thought she could walk no further. The wonderful smell of cooking coming from the inn drew her. She did have the money that Marcus had given her. She wore the money bag tied round her waist under her clothes. She stopped behind a wall and took out one of the gold guineas.

When she pushed open the inn door the men stopped talking, looking at her. But she had eyes only for the tray of pies still steaming hot from the oven.

A large women behind the bar shouted at her. "Get out of here. We don't want any beggars." When she didn't move the woman advanced on her. She had huge arms like legs of beef. She almost lifted Serena off her feet to throw her out. "Please, please I have money. I can pay for a pie." The woman let her go, surprised at the refined accent coming from a tinker.

One kindly man stepped forward. "Come on Jessie. Give the girl a chance. I'll buy her a pie. She looks as though she could do with eating something." Serena thanked him. "You are very kind sir but you see I do have money." She held up the gold sovereign. "Put it away quickly." The man said. "People have been killed for much less than that. You go and sit at a table. I'll get you a pie and maybe some milk."

No sooner had he left than a weasel looking man sidled up to the table. "Are you all alone my dear?" When Serena nodded he pulled out a chair. "You are a very lucky young girl to have all that money." Serena made to get up. He caught her arm. "Now don't be so hasty. I could walk with you wherever you are going. It's not safe for a young girl to be alone." Hardly were the words out of his mouth when Jessie came rushing over. In one swoop she caught him by the scruff of the neck. "You have been warned before. Scrounging off customers. And maybe worse. A lot of people have been robbed when you are around." He cursed and spluttered. "Get your hands off me. I was doing no harm." "That's as maybe but I don't want you in here again.." And with one heave of her mighty arms he was thrown onto the road.

"That's a bad man. You be careful when you leave. He could be hanging about." He placed the steaming pie and milk on the table. Serena wolfed them down. The men looking at her thought, the girl is half starved yet she had enough money for food.

He sensed a mystery. "Where are you bound for?" He asked. Serena thought where on earth was she bound for. She thought quickly. "Oh to the next town." She told him. "Oh that will be Bridgetown. Quite a bit away. I am the driver of the coach out by. I can give you a lift for part of the way." "Thank you sir for all your kindness." She slept as the coach travelled mile after mile. It was the coach stopping that woke her. The coach man called to her. "We are at the crossroads. This is as far as I can take you. I go to the next village. You are only a few miles away from Bridgetown. I wish you well my dear."

Serena stood at the side of the road watching the coach disappear. She felt so lost and lonely. Then she told herself once again. Stop feeling sorry for yourself. You have food in your stomach, another pie and cheese from kind Jessie in the inn. Not only that she had money. She would not be hungry as she was when she travelled the roads with her father. Thinking about him she remembered that his painting of the lady in the yellow dress had been left behind. She wondered what would happen to it but she still had the painting of Shannon house.

Chapter 8

S he walked for miles along the rough dusty road. Rounding a corner suddenly the sea came into view. She felt her spirits lifting. She realised just how much she missed it. She made her way down some steps to a beautiful sandy cove sheltered on each side by the rocks. She couldn't resist. There was no one around. She took off her cloak, skirt and bodice leaving on her chemise and petticoat and waded into the sea. As she swam around all the aches and pains left her. Her poor feet felt soothed. After a while she started to feel tired and made her way behind the rocks. She spread out her cloak and lay down to let the sun dry her. She remembered the pie that Jessie had given her. When she ate it she felt herself falling asleep. Her last thought was dear whispering sea I get so much pleasure from you.

She awoke with a start. It was the laughter of a small boy playing with his ball on the sand that had wakened her. A man was sitting reading not far from where she was lying. She crept around looking for her clothes. Something made her look towards the sea. The child was wading out trying to reach his ball which was floating out of his reach.

The man, deep in his book, hadn't noticed the danger the child was in. She screamed at him and pointed to the sea. The man, surprise on his face at the sudden appearance of a young girl screaming at him, then horror as he realised where she was pointing. Serena raced in and was just in time to grab the child as it sunk into the sea, the water closing over it's head. She gathered him up in her arms. He was lying limp. She laid him on the sand and started to pump his chest the way her father had taught her. You never know when it might be needed he had told her. The child gave a shudder and coughed up the sea water he had swallowed. He started to cry. Serena turned to the man. "You better get him home quickly."

He gathered the child in his arms and turned to Serena. "Thank God you were here. This is Sam my nephew. Our house is just along the lane. You must come with us to get dried. And look, you are shivering." He looked at her for the first time. He caught his breath. He had never seen anyone so perfectly lovely. Her long dark hair, soaked, clung to her body, partly concealing it. The clothing, flimsy, done little to hide the beauty of her young body, her breasts pushing against it with it's rose tipped nipples.

Serena, quite unaware of her near nakedness, smiled at him. "Thank you. I'll just collect my things. I would like to see this young man settled at home."

They climbed up to the road. Serena noticed for the first time that steps led to the beach. As if reading her thoughts the man explained that the little cove was private. "It belongs to Sam's parents."

"So I was trespassing?" Serena said. "I am sorry." "Don't be sorry. Thank God that some providence made you go there to save Sam's life."

Round the corner a pony and trap were waiting, the pony quite content, chewing the grass. The three of them bundled in. "The house is just around the corner. We could have walked here but Sam loves the pony and trap. He sits on my knee holding the reins. He thinks he is the driver. But today my poor old man you will have to sit on this young lady's knee."

The house was indeed just round the corner. Serena's first impression was square, a square house. Large, three storied, it stood on a flat piece of ground. The lawns it seemed to Serena that not one piece of grass was allowed to spoil the perfect manicure. The flower beds from the entrance gates ran in straight lines to the large front door. The door opened as they arrived. A tall grim faced woman stood there. "Oh help." The man said. "That's Mrs Petters, the housekeeper. I'm in trouble. I was supposed to make sure that Sam had his afternoon nap. But it was such a lovely day I thought why not let the little fellow have some fun instead of being stuck away in a nursery."

The woman was glaring at Serena and no wonder. Serena thought she must have looked a terrible sight.

Quickly the man turned to Serena. "In all that's been happening I haven't asked your name." "It's Serena Church. And your name sir?" She asked. "It's Ben Wallace. Sam's father is my brother. Come now I must introduce you. Explanations can come later. We must get Sam into bed." He carried Sam, pushing Mrs Petters aside, saying over his shoulder to her. "This is Serena. Please find a room for her. As you can see she needs to get changed."

Serena followed the stiff backed housekeeper up two flights of stairs to, Serena presumed, was the servants quarters. She turned to Serena. "I will of course have to report this carry on to the master Mr Wallace. Lucky for you Mrs Wallace is away for a few days. One of the maids will bring you water to wash."

Serena looked round the room. Bare floor boards. Not even a rug. A single iron bed and a chest of drawers with a bit of a cracked mirror. She wished she was back out lying by the sea.

There was knock at the door. A young girl of about ten was carrying a basin and a jug of water. "Cook said that when you are ready you have to come to the kitchen to get some food. I'm Elsie. I work in the scullery doing the pots." The child seemed to want to linger. Serena had to ease her out the door. She was desperate to get out of her wet underclothes. She washed hurriedly. Thankfully she had managed, in the rush to get away from Marcus's, to stuff some things to change into her bag.

She made her way down the stairs looking for the kitchen. There seemed to be endless corridors. Eventually she followed the smell of cooking. She opened the kitchen door and stepped into such a homely scene after the gloomy dark corridors. A plump rosy cheeked woman was standing by a large range stirring something that smelt like stew. It made Serena realise how hungry she was.

"Come on in my dear. Sit you down at the table with the others. I'll soon get you fed."

Serena turned round. Sam's uncle was sitting at the table with two of the servant girls tucking into a large plate of stew. Serena looked at him. He really was handsome. Twinkling blue eyes, thick dark hair tied back with a length of thin ribbon. He was much younger than she first thought.

"Come in Serena." He pulled out a chair for her. "You have already met Elsie. And this cheeky one is Mary the housemaid." Mary, a plump freckle faced girl grinned at him. "Oh you are a card sir."

He turned to Serena. "Are you feeling better? You were really shivering I think maybe with shock." "Yes thank you. I am fine. Tell me. How is Sam?" "Oh he is fine. Sound asleep. You can see him when he wakens up."

Serena felt so relaxed sitting there in the homely kitchen. When she had finished eating Ben took her to meet his brother. "He will be in the study. He spends most of the day there." They went down more corridors but this time they were bright and beautifully carpeted. Ben opened the study door. "Ian I have a visitor for you."

Serena was taken aback. The man who turned to greet them looked like an old man with a mane of white hair and stooped shoulders. He held out his hand to Serena. "Welcome my dear and thank God you were there to save my son." He smiled and immediately he looked years younger. "I hope you are taking care of her Ben. Why don't you stay for a few days Serena. That's if you are not in a hurry to get anywhere." Serena thought to herself why not. She felt safe here. "Thank you sir. I would like that." She told him. "Good, good." He said. "Now I must get on with my work." He turned back to a large desk covered with papers. They were dismissed.

Serena felt taken aback at his rudeness. "Don't worry about my brother. He doesn't mean to be rude. He owns a cotton mill and lately he has had a lot of worries. He has had to get a lot of new machinery to keep up with the competitors. Cheaper cotton is coming in from abroad. I'm afraid that I am of little help to him. I know nothing of the business."

"What do you do?" Serena asked. He smiled at her. "I can tell you that I am just a layabout sitting on the beach all day. Well my dear you are wrong. I have always loved being around horses and when the parents died I invested the money left to me in buying stables just outside the town. If you are still here Serena I would like to take you there. I'm very proud of them. Come on now. I'll take you up to see Sam. He should be awake now."

When they entered the nursery Sam was wide awake. He stretched out his arms to Ben and when he lifted him up on to his shoulders he squealed with delight. Ben washed his face and hands. "Come on now young man. Let's go to the kitchen and see if cook has something nice for you to eat."

He turned to Serena. "Sam loves going to the kitchen. My sister in law does not approve. He usually has all his meals in the nursery." "Is Sam's mother strict with him?" "Well I don't know if you would call it strict. Sometimes I think she is almost uncaring, leaving his upbringing to whoever happens to be around. Usually the servants. Yes I'm afraid my sister in law Olga is a very self centred person."

The next two days Serena enjoyed wandering around the house and having such friendly company when she went to the kitchen for meals. She saw very little of Mrs Petters. When she did meet her she just sniffed and glared at her, never speaking.

It was on the morning of her third day in the house. She was sitting at the kitchen table with Ben when there was a loud commotion outside the door. It was Mrs Petter's voice yelling at Mary the housemaid. "You will do as you are told. These rooms have got to be cleaned. The mistress is coming back tomorrow with some of her friends. You are bone lazy." Mary was shouting back at her. "I can't clean the whole house. You are asking too much. I'm leaving. You shouldn't have got rid of the other girls that worked here. You thought you were clever, keeping in with the mistress, saving her money."

"You won't get a reference from me." Mrs Petters was yelling. "I won't need one." Mary yelled back. "I'm going to work for my aunt at the inn. She has been wanting me to work there for some time."

She came flying into the kitchen, banging the door when Mrs Petters made to follow her.

"Come here Mary." Cook rose and put her arms round her. "Don't upset yourself. We know you are a good worker. Maybe Mrs Petters will calm down and try to get someone else to help you. I'll make you a nice cup of tea. Don't be too hasty Mary about leaving."

It didn't take Mrs Petters long to realise the mistake she had made upsetting Mary. She desperately needed her help. There was such a lot to do. Not only were there rooms to get ready but Mary always helped to serve when there was a large number for dinner. She racked her brains for a solution to the problem. Then suddenly inspiration struck her. What about that girl Serena? She seemed to be doing nothing, prowling about the house, sitting in the kitchen, eating good meals. Why couldn't she help Mary for a few days?

She straightened her shoulders and marched into the kitchen. "That didn't take long." Cook murmured to herself. "I think we shall forget our differences Mary. I would be obliged if you would stay." She turned to Serena. "Do you think you would be able to help Mary for a few days?" Before she could reply Ben spoke up. "Now Mrs Petters. Serena is our guest. I think you are quite out of order suggesting such a thing." Mrs Petters flushed with anger ready to reply when Serena spoke up.

Of course I will help but I will need you to help me Mary." Mary was hesitating. Mrs Petters, determined not to let this opportunity pass, turned to Mary. "Of course I will increase your salary." "By how much?" Mary demanded. "I will have a word with the master." She said. "He can decide." So peace was restored and Serena had a job and a safe place to stay. There was little chance that anyone from Crawford would find her here.

The next day was so busy she didn't think she had ever worked so hard. With Mary

guiding her she turned large feather mattresses, washed curtains and after drying them outside, worked till nearly midnight ironing them. Wooden floors were scrubbed and polished. When all the bedrooms were finished they had to start in the large lounge dusting and building up the fires. In the whole house there was a hive of activity. Cook in the kitchen was moaning. "I don't know how many guests I have to cook for. The mistress has no consideration." And by her tone Serena guessed that cook was not too fond of the mistress.

Late afternoon the coaches started to arrive. Serena watching from an upstairs window counted eighteen guests. A great deal of laughing and joking as they were taken to their rooms.

There was no sign of Mr Wallace. It was Ben who met them A perfect host. He really was a charming man Serena thought.

A small fair haired woman was giving orders. "That's Mrs Wallace." Mary said from behind her.

Serena thought she had never seen anyone so pretty with her beautiful pale pink dress showing off her beautiful complexion. She looked like a china doll she had seen in a book. Ian was talking to her as they made their way into the lounge. He must have been telling her about Sam's accident because shortly afterwards Mrs Petters came to look for Serena. "The mistress wants to see you in the lounge."

Serena was horrified. She felt so dirty. Her hair had escaped from her cap and was tumbling down her back. Mary looked at her. With her borrowed clothes that were far too big for her she still looked beautiful.

Mary took her hand. "Serena you must listen to me. The mistress is a strange woman. She can't bear anyone around who is better looking than her and she can't bear competition."

"What do you mean competition?" Serena asked. "Never mind." Mary said. "I have said enough. Now get your hair tucked in and keep your head down when she talks to you. Please Serena, take my advice."

Chapter 9

Mary talking to her the way she did did not do anything for Serena's confidence. She barely lifted her head when she entered the lounge. Mrs Wallace was standing by the fire. Ben, standing behind her, winked at her which made her more nervous.

"So you are the heroine. I believe you saved my son's life. Wasn't it as well that you were trespassing on my beach." "I'm sorry about that madam. I had not realised it was private."

Ben coughed. "This young lady Olga has also saved you a lot of embarrassment in front of your guests. She has been working hard with Mary to get the house ready."

Serena thought. I was right thinking she looked like a china doll. Large blue cold looking eyes. Serena's instinct told her that behind the prettiness was a cold selfish woman. She never went to see Sam to check that he was all right.

Ian came into the lounge. "Did you have a nice time my dear?" He turned to Serena. "It is very good of you to help out. We are most grateful to you. Aren't we dear?" Olga smiled at Serena. "Of course we are."

Serena thought. Ian wasn't just stuck in the study all day with his books. He knew everything that was going on in the house.

Serena felt happy working in the house. Everyone took it for granted that she would stay to work there. Mrs Petters was organising a uniform for her. Apart from going to the kitchen for meals she never went downstairs. Mrs Petters gave all the orders. She was glad that she never had to come into contact with Olga Wallace. Ben was about the house a lot. She started to look forward to his company in the kitchen with Sam when Olga wasn't around.

Sam was such an affectionate little boy. He would run to her when he saw her and give her a hug. Once or twice when Serena managed to have a few hours off she would play with him in the back garden, keeping away from the neat rows of vegetables. Down to the overgrown part, where the grass was almost as tall as Sam, he loved to play hide and seek with her and when she pretended to find him he would shriek with laughter.

It was this laughter that attracted Ben. When he had volunteered to bring vegetables in for cook he saw them racing about in the tall grass, Serena's hair loose from her cap, flying about to her waist. Once again as it did that day on the beach he caught his breath at her beauty.

The days passed quickly and even although the work was hard she felt safe there. From the first day of meeting Olga Wallace she never ran into her in the house. Serena's place was upstairs and Olga Wallace took little to do with that part of the house.

Mrs Petters accepted Serena. She realised how lucky she was to have found such a good worker.

Olga Wallace was forever going away for days at a time."She is in with a right fast crowd." Cook said. Serena felt that when she was away a happy atmosphere was in the house. And Ian Wallace in his quiet way was very much the head of the household.

"I can't think why he married Olga." Mary said one day. "Well she is very pretty." Serena said. Mary shrugged. "Oh yes that's as maybe. You know she worked in the office at the mill and she chased the master, determined to get him and then she became pregnant. The master done the decent thing and married her. He more or less lets her have free reign. But when she goes too far he pulls the reigns in. She knows where her bread is buttered but one day she may go too far."

"Everyone knows that she is besotted with Ben." "And does Ben feel the same about her?" Serena asked. "Not him. He thinks it's very funny.

Olga has got nothing to fear from Lizzie or me. We are the plain Janes of the world but you Serena are so lovely. It is as well when the mistress saw you with the cap pulled down over your eyes and your ill fitting clothes you posed no threat in catching Ben's eye. You make sure Serena that she always sees you like that or she would throw you out. She's done it before with a pretty little girl from the village that Mrs Petters hired. The poor girl arrived home in tears. Her parents created quite a row and made the mistress write a good reference for her."

Serena was at her happiest when she played with Sam. And when the mistress was away Ben would join them. If it was a wet day they usually ended up in the kitchen eating cooks lovely buns.

"There won't be any food left in my kitchen." Cook would moan. But she loved having them around. But when she saw how well Serena and Ben got on she looked worried.

The summer was coming to an end. Already the feel of Autumn was in the air. Soon we won't be able to play in the bottom garden. But never mind Sam. Today the sun is shining. We will go there after you have your nap. And make the most of your mother being away she thought to herself. They weren't long in the garden when Ben joined them. Serena had removed her cap and cloak. Ben thought, I could just sit and watch her. Every time I see her she seems to grow more beautiful.

Serena, racing about trying to catch a late summer butterfly, bumped into Ben. He automatically put his arms round her. Serena for a moment rested her head on his chest. She enjoyed the comfort of his arms.

Meantime at the house Mary was horrified to see the mistress arriving home unexpectedly. There was no time to warn Serena. She only hoped she would go straight upstairs but of all times she went to the kitchen. "Cook." She shouted. Cook was sitting by the back door, a bowl of peas on her lap. She was looking down the garden enjoying the laughter coming from Sam.

Olga's voice coming from behind her gave her such a start. She jumped up, the bowl of peas going flying. "What's going on." She demanded. She was just in time to see Ben giving a strange girl a hug. The girl was resting her head on his chest. "Who is that with Sam and Ben?" She demanded, her face red with rage. "Go and fetch them to me in the lounge."

Serena's face lost all it's joy. "Don't let Olga worry you." Ben said. Cook sniffed. She had seen the rage on her face. She went to tuck her hair back under her cap when Ben stopped her. "Leave it Serena. You are off duty. It's none of Olga's business what you do with your hair. And anyway I think it's so beautiful it's a shame to keep it covered all the time."

They made their way to the lounge. Olga looked up when they entered. Ben stepped forward and gave her a peck on the cheek, hoping to mollify her. She brushed him aside and kept staring at Serena. "And who are you?" She asked her. "But ma'am you know me. You hired me a few weeks ago. Remember? The time Sam nearly drowned."

Olga was looking at her in astonishment. This couldn't be the girl that stood before her looking like a scarecrow. This girl was beautiful. Her anger rose. She had been duped. She would never have hired her. And this was the girl that Ben was hugging. She felt like crossing the floor and putting her arms round her neck and choking her. She managed to pull herself together. She couldn't act like that in front of Ben. She would bide her time.

Serena dreading coming face to face with Olga was surprised that when she did meet her she smiled at her. "Are you settling in Serena?" She asked. And when Serena, surprised stammered. "Yes. Thank you madam." She said. "I must get Mrs Petters to hurry getting you a uniform. What you are wearing is not very becoming." And so it went on. Olga being nice to her.

"I have never seen her being nice to any of the servants." Mary said. "I don't trust her. I think she is up to something."

One day she called Serena to her room. She handed her a beautiful silk scarf. "Do take this. I notice that when you take off your cap you have nothing to tie your hair back." "I can't take something so beautiful." Serena felt uncomfortable. Olga pressed it into her hand. "Please take it. Don't tell the staff I gave it to you. I don't want them to be jealous." This made Serena feel worse. She took it and put it into the back of her drawer. "Well the mistress seems to have taken to you Serena." Cook said.

Olga with her constant dinner parties kept the few staff busy from morning till night. Ian, locked away in the study showed little interest in Olga's guests. He seldom put in an appearance. Serena could understand this. They seemed to her to be a rowdy crowd, Olga enjoying the compliments they showered on her.

The day before one of the dinner parties Mary took ill. She had a high temperature with bouts of sickness. She wasn't able to move from her bed. Olga was furious. "What about my dinner party? Who is going to wait at tables?" No sympathy was shown to poor Mary. It was cook's suggestion that Serena should do it. "She is a sensible lass." Olga was in tight spot. The last thing she wanted was to have Serena there in front of her friends but there was no one else.

Serena felt nervous when the time came the next night to serve dinner. She carried in the first course and Olga's worry was justified . When Serena entered, the conversation round the table stopped dead. Then one of the younger men turned to Olga. "Where have you been hiding this beauty?" Then they all started talking to her. Serena turned round in time to see a look of pure hatred on Olga's face. She hurried back to the kitchen. "I can't go back in there cook. I just can't. Why does Olga hate me so?" Cook hugged her. "She hates you because you are lovelier than her and taking all the attention away from her. Now you just go back in there and finish your work." And cook almost snorted. "There can't be any gentleman among that lot to upset a girl even although it was complimentary."

So Serena, head held high, ignored them all. And when she finished she escaped to her room. Cook told her the next day that a number of them had come into the kitchen looking for the lovely table maid. And Olga, when they had gone, in a fit of rage, threw one of the tall ornate vases crashing into the fireplace. The noise brought Ian from the study. "What's happened here? He demanded. "It's your fault. Why did you hire that girl? She made a fool of my dinner party. Flirting with my guests."

Ian looked at her. "Now you know that's not true Olga. The only one misbehaving is you. Watch your step my girl. I have given you full reign with the running of the house and with money because you are Sam's mother. But things are going to change."

Olga realised she had gone too far. She crossed the room and smiling her most seductive smile tried to put her arms round his neck but he pushed her away and walked back to the comfort of the study.

The next day Olga was off on her usual two or three days with her cronies and the whole household breathed a sigh of relief. When she returned she was very quiet and stayed mostly in her room.

Chapter 10

I an and Ben were having business meetings. Mary said that when she took in their meals they both looked very grave. I think things are going badly at the mill.

A few days afterwards Ian informed the staff that he and Ben would be away for some time. A lot of work had to be done negotiating the price of cotton. "Ben is going with me. He is a better negotiator than I am."

When they had gone Olga was back to her old self. Another big dinner was arranged but this time Mary was able to serve and this time it was older people that were invited. Business men and their over dressed wives, delighted to be invited to the mill owners house. Mrs Petters took them into the lounge. Mary served them drinks.

They were standing around waiting for Olga to put in an appearance when there was a scream from upstairs. The guests rushed to find out what had happened. Olga was standing at the top of the stairs, still shouting and crying.

"I've been robbed. My brooch has gone." Mary tried to calm her. "Maybe you just misplaced it." She pushed her aside. "You stupid girl. This is the most expensive piece of jewellery I have. Ian will be cross. He kept saying I should keep all my jewellery in the bank."

A pompous man stepped forward. "If it's in the house we will find it. When did you last see it?" "Well only the other day I was showing it to the new servant girl. I was asking her advice about wearing it tonight. As you can see my dress is very plain. The brooch would have set it off." There was a murmur from the guests. The pompous man said. "Why don't we talk to this girl?"

Serena, so far from the rest of the house, hadn't heard any of the commotion. She was surprised when Olga marched into her room followed by the guests. Olga, all sweetness, explained. "Sorry about this intrusion Serena but my brooch has been stolen or lost. We are searching the whole house." Serena's face paled. She knew at once what Olga had been planning. It didn't take long to search Serena's bare little room. Then the pompous man gave a cry. "Is this it?" He held the brooch high. "Yes yes that's it. Oh Serena how could you. And look there is my scarf. You are a wicked girl stealing from me after all the kindness I have shown you."

Serena just stood. Too shaken to speak or move. Someone in the crowd said they would go for the magistrate. Lock her in the room till he arrives.

To Serena the next few hours were a nightmare. No one believed her when she said Olga had given these things to her. Even Mary was looking at her puzzled. She suddenly felt so tired repeating the same thing over and over. She still felt numb and tired when she was taken to the cells and to appear in court in the morning charged with theft. Who was going to take her word against Olga's. She was taken into the court. Mary, cook, even Elsie were there. They asked if they could speak for her but it was of no avail.

But maybe the sight of Serena looking pale and almost unreal in her fragile beauty softened the magistrate's heart and he gave her the smallest sentence he could of six months in prison.

To Serena she would have preferred death. To be locked away from all the things she loved. Running about with Sam in the tall grass. Walking in the moonlight with the frost sparkling in the grass. But most of all running into the sea. All her happy memories were associated with the sea. Her dear whispering sea. It was as if everything that was happening to her was like in some nightmare. She was stripped and put into a shower by a grim faced woman. Then a coarse gown slipped over her head. She was told to sit on a stool. Before she could take in what was happening the woman produced a large pair of scissors and proceeded to cut her hair. She felt faint when she saw large lengths of her hair lying on the floor. She put her hand up to her head. All that was left of her hair was cut close to her scalp.

She was handed a towel and a blanket and ushered into a cell. Only then did she realise what was happening to her. There was no one to help her. Ben and Ian Wallace were away. Olga had timed everything well.

She crawled into the bed her whole body shaking with sobs.

"So you had your hair chopped. Not a very good hairdresser the Bulldog." Serena turned. She hadn't noticed anyone under the blanket in the other bed. She was a thin slip of a girl not older than about fourteen she thought. But she had an old face.

"My name is Amy. What's yours?" She asked. When Serena told her she sniffed. "Very posh. It goes with your voice. That's posh too. What are you doing in here? Oh don't tell me. It's a mistake. Your innocent."

Serena started to cry again. Even this child woman thought she must be guilty of something. "Here, don't go on so. I can't stand anyone blubbering. I'm in for shop lifting. A year the old fart gave me. But I must admit it was my third offence. What was I to do. I couldn't let my young brother and sister starve."

"What about your parents? Serena asked. "Couldn't they look after them?"

Amy shrugged her thin shoulders. "All we got from them was a clip round the ear. They drank every penny they could lay their hands on.

Serena was amazed. She had never come across any one like Amy. A voice bellowed at them from the next cell. "Stop nattering in there. Some of us want to sleep."

As the days passed Serena thanked God for the friendship of Amy.

She was just like a little terrier when some of the women tried to bully her. They felt that she was different. Not like them. They all had work to do. It went on from daybreak till dusk. Serena was allocated to the kitchen. Amy was already working there. At least, Serena thought, I can help this poor thin girl lifting heavy pots and standing for hours at a time peeling mountains of potatoes.

Serena thought she could stand anything if only she could go outside just to be in the fresh air. Then the second day, the part of the cell she was in was allowed outside for an hour. Apparently there were too many to allow all the prisoners out at the same time and on the same day.

Serena was overjoyed. She turned her face to the sky and breathed in fresh air. "What a bloody fuss." Amy said. "Over a bit of air. I got plenty of air when the parents chucked me out. Oh yes the air isn't so good when you are freezing with the cold lying in a doorway."

Serena thought back to all the times she had felt cold and hungry. But never as bad as Amy. Her father always tried to find shelter and not only that she had his company. It seemed that poor Amy had nothing. Maybe prison gave her the comfort she never got on the outside.

It was the dreary existence that got the prisoners down. There was nothing for them to do but work. As a result lots of fights and arguments broke out over the smallest things. Amy managed to steer her clear of them.

There was excitement one day among the prisoners. A new crowd of prisoners were getting transferred from another prison. Everyone was hanging over the rails outside the cells looking to see if there was anyone they knew.

Serena, not paying much attention, looked down at the new arrivals. Then the blood seemed to freeze in her veins. She was looking at the face of Isa Jones. Just then, Isa, looking around, stared for a moment at Serena. She looked away, a puzzled look on her face. Then they were all taken away. Serena breathed a sigh of relief. She hadn't recognised her. And maybe the new arrivals would be taken to another part of the prison and Isa Jones would never meet her.

So much for all her hope. The very next day, walking down the corridor, they came face to face and this time there was no doubt. A cruel smile on her face told Serena that she was in for a hard time.

In no time she had gathered some of the nastiest prisoners round her. Even the Bulldog seemed to let them off with all their bullying of some of the gentler prisoners like poor Amy.

There was loud laughter from her cronies when she tipped over the large pot of potatoes that Serena had just finished peeling. And when the Bulldog made her start peeling another pot full Serena bit her lip to stop herself from crying knowing that she wouldn't be getting an hour outside. Amy held her arm. "I'll stay Serena and do the potatoes. You go out. You know I'm not that keen on flaming fresh air."

Day after day the torment went on. Each morning everyone had to empty their slop buckets. Serena standing in the queue waiting to empty hers felt someone push against her. She turned for a split second. She saw Isa Jones' face leering at her. Then horror of horrors, the contents of a slop bucket covered her from head to foot. Even Bulldog had a look of horror on her face. She had seen who the culprit was but later when the incident came to the attention of the warden she denied seeing anything.

Loud laughter and shouting coming from the washroom drew Serena's attention. The Bulldog was standing outside the door making no attempt to go in to discover what it was about. When Serena tried to go in she barred her path. "Get back to your work." Something made Serena shove her out of the way. When she entered the room all she saw was a circle of the prisoners, each taking a turn to kick a bundle of clothes from one to another. Then she nearly fainted with horror. The bundle of clothes lifted a head from her curled up body. It was Amy and Isa Jones was egging them on.

Serena never quite remembered what happened next. Someone was trying to pull her off Isa Jones. She remembered through a red haze trying to kill her. She half lifted half carried Amy to the cell and shouted at the Bulldog to get a doctor. Amy was taken to the prison hospital and she had broken ribs and her body was covered in bruises. After a couple of days she was back in the cell. The only reason for her getting such a beating was because of her friendship with Serena.

The Governor heard the story of what had happened. Bulldog was taken to his office and whatever happened there she was seen leaving. Kicked out someone said.

In no time Amy was back to her tough little person. She was one of the world's survivors.

For Serena it was different. How could I have attacked another human being she kept asking Amy. Amy hugged her. "Oh Serena. If you hadn't done so I think I might have been killed."

Things changed in the prison. All the followers that Isa Jones had had transferred their attention to Serena. It was as though they looked up to someone as tough or tougher than themselves. Isa Jones was now getting a taste of her own medicine. She tried to get in with Serena but she kept her at a distance. She couldn't forgive her for all the misery she had caused her. Because of her and another bitter, jealous woman, Olga Wallace, she had ended up here, barely eighteen years of age.

At night as she tossed and turned, her thoughts went back to the happier time of her life when she and her father had made a little home on the beach. And with it the remembrance of James, shy and embarrassed when instead of kissing her on the cheek his lips had found hers. A kiss she would remember all her life.

Some weeks had passed since the episode of the fight in the washroom. Serena was escorted to the Governor's office. She was shaking with nerves.

They passed down numerous corridors. The guard knocked at a large oak door. It was opened by what seemed to Serena to be a servant. He wore some sort of uniform. He ushered Serena in and told the guard to wait outside. When he shut the door he took her into a pleasant room. At a large table near the middle of the floor four men were seated. At the top of the table a severe looking man was looking at her when she entered.

"You are Serena Church? He said. And Serena felt confused because his voice was soft and gentle. Later Serena was told that in spite of the soft voice he could be harsh in his judgements.

The four men at the table took it in turns to ask her questions. Not one of them asked if she was innocent of the crime she was charged with because after all the charge had been made and the sentence made.

After a few minutes the man at the top of the table, Serena realised, was the Governor. Of course there had been no introductions. He was the Governor and she was a prisoner. He beckoned to the man who had brought her in and she was escorted back out of the room.

Two days later she was told that she was free to go. She had completed three months of her sentence. She never knew such joy. To be free to walk in the sun. To feel the rain and wind in her face. In spite of her joy she felt sad at leaving young Amy who still had a lot of her sentence to finish because it wasn't the first offence she had committed.

Their farewells were tearful. "I won't forget you ever." Amy managed a tearful smile. Serena hugged her. "I will never forget you Amy and I promise that someday we will meet again." She collected and signed for her pitiful possessions. She had been taken in with only the clothes she stood in.

The big doors banged behind her. She was free. It was a cold miserable November day but she didn't mind. She stood and gulped in the wonderful air.

"Serena, Serena." A voice was shouting from across the road. Serena looked. It was Mary her dear friend. They hugged and cried. "How did you know Mary that I was getting out today?" "It was Ian Wallace. He came to tell me to go and meet you. It was Ian's help that got you released. He knew important people who pulled strings. Things changed after you were arrested. I couldn't work there anymore. I work now at my aunt's guest house. In fact she suggested that you come home with me."

Serena shook her head. "Dear Mary you are so kind but I would prefer to travel on."

Mary produced a pack. "Look Serena. Ian Wallace gave me money to buy you clothes and boots. He is a good man. He managed to save the mill by releasing all his assets including the big house. Olga and Sam moved into a small house, only keeping on Elsie because he knew she would find it difficult getting a place. Olga had to do most of the housework herself. He put an end to all her extravagances.

Ben felt that he was partly to blame for what happened to you. He sold up the stables and went back to sea. We believe that he helped Ian to save the mill. As soon as you were taken away Olga made a bonfire of all your things. I managed to save a few things including a picture that you seemed to love. It's the one of a beautiful mansion house and

Gardens. It is all rolled up in the pack."

"Oh Mary. How kind you are. How can I ever repay you?" Then Serena had a sudden thought. "What about my cape? Did you manage to save it?" "Well I almost managed but one side was so badly burnt. I knew you wouldn't wear it so I gave it to an old gypsy woman who came begging at the door." Serena smiled and thought. I hope that she finds the money sewn into the hem.

Mary tried to hide her shock at Serena's appearance. Her hair, beginning to grow in still stuck up like sheaves in a cornfield. Her skin had a yellow tinge. But thank God Mary thought, she still had the proud posture, her head held high. Whatever happens to this child. Yes she thought, a child. She will come though it.

She handed her the pack and from over her arm she took a thick wool cloak. She placed it round Serena, gave her a quick hug, turned and almost ran away. She didn't want Serena to see her in tears.

Serena stood and watched her till she was out of sight, then she threw back her shoulders. "Well Serena." She said to herself. "It's you alone in the world." The rain fell on her face. She smiled.

Chapter 11

Weeks had passed since she heard the bang of the prison doors behind her. She had refused Mary's help. She had to escape to put miles behind all that had happened to her.

To begin with she thought she wouldn't be able to survive. She shivered with the cold at night. She felt so weak she could barely walk more than two or three miles. But gradually her youth and natural resilience took over and she started to remember all the tips her father had taught as they wandered the country. It was the worst time of year to be out. She had to face everything. Sleet, winds and severe white frosts. Sometimes not even a rock that she could lay beside. It was a cold barren part of the country. She thanked God for the warm cloak. She would dig out a shallow trench and cover herself from head to foot with it.

One late afternoon the darkness was coming down quickly. She felt the first few flakes of snow. She looked around. No shelter anywhere. It would have to be in a trench. She found a stone and dug until it would take her length. She lay down and covered herself with the cloak. It was surprising how warm it was with the fine coating of snow covering her.

She managed to doze fitfully. She had been exhausted. She had walked many miles. It was early dawn. Still just a half light. She rose up slowly and she nearly jumped out of her skin when just in front of her a man was screaming in absolute terror. Scream after scream came from him and when Serena went to touch him he collapsed at her feet.

"I'll never steal again. Don't take me. Please don't take me. Here you have it." He threw a bundle at Serena's feet and half crawled and half ran away from her, still muttering to himself. "I'll never steal again. That was death coming for me."

When Serena got over the shock and realised what had happened she sat on the ground laughing till her sides ached. The poor man. No wonder he got a shock. I rose out of the ground just at his feet covered in snow. He believed that death had come for him.

Now what had he been stealing. Serena opened the bundle. There was a large cheese, bread, a cask of wine, a silver plate and a candlestick. It was all wrapped in a large table cloth. It was as if he had just cleared a whole table and it looked as if it might have come from a big house.

Serena was in a quandary. The food it seemed was like a gift from heaven. But what to do with the bits of silver. If she was found with it she could be sent back to prison. She made her decision. She packed away the food in her bag and wrapped the silver in the tablecloth and left it by the road where it could be found. Quickly she started walking away as far from it as she could. She still felt herself chuckling, remembering the poor thief who thought his time had come.

It seemed to Serena that she had been walking all her life. She longed to lay her head down on a real bed. She reckoned that it would soon be Christmas and remembering the happiness she had shared with her father, she felt the tears welling up. She shook herself. Come now Serena. Stop feeling sorry for yourself. It is better by far wandering the roads than waking up in a prison cell. Apart from drinking water from the near frozen streams she had had nothing to eat for two or three days. The food that the thief had flung at her was long gone. She was beginning to feel faint and once or twice she stumbled. It seemed that she was alone in the world. She had not met anyone for days and when she did see the light shining brightly from a farmhouse she couldn't believe it.

The light from the window drew her like a magnet. A family were seated round the fire. A man, woman and three children. The youngest child, a little girl of about three, was perched on the man's knee. He seemed to be telling her a story. Now and then he would stroke her hair and Serena noticed his hands, so rough and calloused, were so gentle.

A boy of about nine was busy carving a piece of wood, deep concentration on his face. The third child, a girl of nine or ten was sitting at the woman's feet while she brushed her hair. The girl said something to the woman which caused a burst of laughter.

To Serena, standing outside in the cold, it felt happy being a witness to such love and happiness coming from that room. She must have made some movement for in a trice the man put down the child and came running outside.

"Who are you?" He demanded. "Why are you looking in our window?" Serena couldn't reply. She felt herself falling and getting lifted up and the next thing she knew the woman was getting her to drink something warm and sweet. "The poor girl." She was saying. Serena thought she had never heard such a beautiful gentle voice. Her face matched the voice. Smiling brown eyes, rosy cheeks, dimpled when she smiled.

Chapter 12

"Please forgive me." She whispered. "I saw the light after walking miles in the darkness."

"Where were you going?" The man demanded. "I don't know. I am looking for work. How far away is the next village?"

The man and woman exchanged glances. There was something not quite right. A young beautiful girl with such a refined accent walking on the moor. It was a dangerous place even in daylight. So many homeless, shiftless people around, prepared to steal to survive.

The youngest member of the family, the little girl, reached over and took her hand. "Poor lady. You are tired. You can come to sleep in my bed. Can't she Ma? Can't she Da?

"I don't think your bed will be big enough Grace but we will find a place for her." The child jumped up and down her fair curls dancing and her big blue eyes smiling. "You are my new friend." She said to Serena. "My name is Grace. What's yours?" And so the decision was made by a little child and for the first time in weeks Serena slept in a real bed. It didn't matter that it was in a corner of the kitchen. After all it was just a makeshift bed for one night.

She awoke with a start the next morning with one of the dogs licking her face. She sprang up. It seemed to be well into the morning. Not a soul around.

Just then the woman came in. She was carrying a pail of milk. "Did you have a good sleep my dear? We tried not to waken you. They will all be trooping in shortly for breakfast."

Soon the kitchen was full of noise. Even little Grace was up and dressed. They all sat round a large table. "Come along lass. There is a place for you." Serena shyly sat down and let her plate be filled with food that she had only imagined. A large slice of pork surrounded by eggs and fat sausages. Fresh baked bread still warm from the oven. There was little talking. Then when everyone had eaten the man stood up. "Now Serena, I think we better introduce ourselves. I am Seth Brown." And he smiled at the woman. "And this bonny woman is my wife Beth." He put his hand on the boy's shoulder who was blushing with embarrassment. "This is my son Jack. And this young lady (who looked so much like her mother) is Sally. Now my dear, Seth continued. We have decided that if it suits you, you could make your home with us and help with the work about the farm. We couldn't afford to pay you much. Times are hard. It seemed they all held their breath, waiting for her reply. "Oh please yes. Thank you." She stuttered and burst into tears. "Don't cry." Little Grace said, climbing onto her knee, dabbing her tears like a little old woman.

A little room above the barn was to be hers. Beth and Sally helped her scrub it out, mother and daughter enjoying finding bits and pieces. An old chest of drawers rescued from the hen house scrubbed and painted. Jack came home lugging an old iron bedstead that had been used to patch a hole in a fence. And so it went on. In the evening sitting round the fire, Beth produced a large piece of canvass and a large bag of rags. "Now children we are going to make a rug for Serena's room. Each of us can take a corner and it can be finished in no time.

Serena was puzzled. She had never heard of such a thing. A rug made out of rags. "I want to help." Little Grace demanded. "Of course you can." Her mother said. "You can pick out all the nice colours." When Seth came in they were all busy. He picked up a bright green shirt from the rags. "I was looking for it. It's my favourite." Beth laughed and snatched it back. "Just look at it Seth. It's full of holes. You looked just like a tinker in it." "Oh well." He said. "It's been put to good use."

Serena soon got the knack of weaving strips of rags of all colours into the canvass. When it was finished she couldn't believe how pretty it looked.

The Winter was passing quickly an now the hard work was beginning on the farm. It became Serena's job to take the produce to the market. Eggs, cheese and bread was loaded onto a cart. Later there would be potatoes and all manner of vegetables. This was all Beth's department while Seth, with the help of one of the local men, ploughed the fields and took care of the livestock.

Serena couldn't believe how her life had changed. She loved this family dearly. They never questioned her about her life before coming to them out of the darkness. Everyone worked, even young Jack. His job was to clear the stones from the ground ready for the plough to go in. He only worked for a short time each day. His mother made sure of that.

When she thought he had done enough she would stand at the bottom of the field waving a cloth like a flag. "Seth doesn't mean to be unkind." She explained to Serena. "But he is a bit thoughtless and he would have Jack working all day."

The days passed so quickly. Such happy days. Sally would accompany her on market day to help her set up the stall. Soon she got to know the people in the village and the farm people from around the area of Oakfield.

"They seem to have taken to you Serena. Normally they can be quite a closed community, not liking strangers, but who could resist you Serena. You are growing more lovely every day."

This was true. The hair that had been chopped had grown in long and luxurious, falling to below her waist. Because of the good food her skin glowed. "The young men of the village will be queuing up to court you."

One day when walking past the village hall with Sally they saw some people looking at a notice that was pinned up. They went over to look. "Oh Serena what does it say?" Sally was pulling her forward. Serena looked at her shocked. Sally couldn't read. Then looking around the village she realised that there wasn't a school.

"Well Sally the notice says that there is going to be a dance. A rose dance and they want help to decorate the hall. Sally clapped her hands. "Oh Serena how wonderful." Soon the whole village was involved. All the hard working farmers took time off. The hall was covered from ceiling to floor with roses made out of paper. Everyone looked out their best clothes. The night of the dance the whole family piled into the cart. "I have never danced." Serena wailed. "Don't worry about that my dear. There will be plenty offers to teach you." Beth said.

And this turned out to be true. "What a wonderful night." Serena said. "Yes and you were the belle of the ball." Seth replied. "Even the old man himself Sir John Barry. He owns all the farms round about including ours, wanted to dance with you."

"How does that work?" Serena wanted to know. "How could any one person own so much?" "Well." Seth tried to explain. "We are tenants. We have agreements. We pay a feu to Sir John. He is very fair. Some landowners are quite prepared to evict tenants if for instance they have maybe had poor harvests or their cattle picked up some kind of trouble like foot and mouth and have to be slaughtered." For a moment Seth looked worried. "Sir John is going to sell the estate. Goodness knows what the new owners will be like."

"Come now Seth cheer up." Beth scolded him. "Yes you're right lass. Let's have a song from everyone."

It was a memory that Serena knew she would never forget. All seated in the old cart singing their hearts out while the old horse plodded along the moonlit road home.

Chapter 13

Serena made a point of talking to Sally when they were alone. "Have you never wanted to read and write Sally?" She hung her head. "It never worried me when I was little but now I wish I could. You are so clever Serena. The way you read the notice about the rose dance. Not many my age in the village know how to read and write. My mum and dad know a little but not enough to teach me and Jack."

"Would you like me to help you and Jack? It was my father who taught me." Sally's face lit up. "Oh that would be great." Then her face clouded over. "We wouldn't have time. We have got to do all our chores." "Well we will have to think of a way. Remember I am here now helping with some of your chores. Maybe we could manage some nights after supper."

That night Serena talked it over with Beth and Seth. "I could just teach them the basics. It really would help them as they get older. Seth wasn't too sure. "Well lass Beth and myself have managed so far without your learning." "But just think about it Seth." Beth said. "You know that when you get in all the accounts you have to go to the minister to read them to you." "Aye lass that's true. Happens you and I could start learning a bit as well."

Jack kicked up a fuss. "I don't want to learn to write. None of my friends can. They will think I'm a sissy." But gradually he came round and surprised them all how quickly he learned. The routine went on for weeks. They couldn't manage every night because work on the farm came first.

One afternoon they had a visit from the minister. It was when they were all at the table having lunch. Beth panicked when she saw him approaching. "I haven't baked a cake. There is nothing but bread and jam to have with his tea."

"Sorry to disturb you at your meal. I won't keep you long." He smiled at Serena. "It's this young lady I want to talk to." Serena paled. The thought that maybe some bad person had accused her of something and she would be taken off to prison again was the first thought that came into her head.

But the minister was still smiling at her. "I believe that you are fluent at reading and writing?" "Yes." Seth said. "She certainly is. She has even managed to put something into my head."

"Well." The minister continued. "How would you like to teach some of the village children?"

Serena was taken aback. She didn't know how to answer. "But where would I teach them?" She recovered, remembering that the village did not have a school.

The minister looked at Seth and Beth. "You know that the manse has got a lot of rooms, some of them never used. Well Sir John and I had a discussion and one of the big downstairs rooms could be turned into a classroom. Sir John has promised to supply all the necessary furniture, books etc. Now what do you think about it Serena? You would of course be paid a small wage from the council.

"But I can't leave Seth and Beth. They have been so kind to me."

"Now now." Seth put in. "Of course you must take it. You can still help out here." "Yes of course." The minister put in. "It will only be for two or three hours maybe a few days a week because all the children need to help out. Most of them will be from the farms round about."

So it was decided that Serena would take on the job of teacher. She went the next day with Beth to look at the room in the manse. It was indeed a large room. It just seemed to be used for all sorts of discarded bits and pieces. "Well we will soon get this sorted out." Beth said starting there and then.

Serena hugged herself with excitement. She was going to be a teacher. Thank you dear father for all you done for me, remembering all the teaching he gave her with such patience and love.

Chapter 14

Within a few days all the furniture that Sir John promised had arrived. The day of the school opening arrived. Serena felt nervous. Was she doing the right thing? Would she be able to teach a room full of children? And then the next thought. What if the children never came? She need not have worried. Before she had time to ring the school bell the children had started to flock in. The parents seemed to be just as excited as the children, standing outside the manse, pride on their faces that their children were going to read and write.

The minister's wife, a small timid looking woman with mousy brown hair that kept escaping from a snood, stood beside the minister that Serena noticed was quite tall and severe looking. The minister gave a short blessing and his wife, Marieann gave each child an apple. "At your playtime." She said as one child started to bite into hers.

And so the first day as a teacher ended. Serena made her way home to the farm feeling quite exhausted. Sally and Jack had been a great help. They knew all the children and could tell her the ones that were bright and the ones who would need extra help.

As the days went on she noticed that some of the children held back, waiting on her to finish. Sometimes this took quite a while. She had to put everything away to leave the room ready for the next morning. At first she was quite happy to have the children crowding round her as they walked through the village dropping off one or two as they passed their homes. Then she realised that each day when they left the school a group of children always seemed to be behind them. They were about ten or eleven in age and they seemed to be terribly uncared for. Ragged clothes and they looked as if the could do with a good wash. They never spoke but she realised that the school children were afraid of them and that was why they felt safe walking with her. She didn't know what to do about it. Surely it was the parents job to make sure that their children weren't bullied. She spoke to Sally and Jack about it. "Well we just keep away from them. They come from the poorest part of the village. Their parents just let them run wild. They don't have to work out on any farms. The fathers when they do work spend their money on drink."

Serena worried about them. It seemed that it was a bit like what had happened to her at Crawford, though this time she was treated with respect. It was the children who were getting bullied.

Now and then two young children would appear. A boy and a girl of about four or five. They would be pressing their faces to the school window and as soon as she walked out to them they would run off. They were lovely children. The little girl with curly fair hair that would have been lovely if it wasn't dirty and matted. The little boy had the same hair. They were obviously brother and sister with the same strange elfin like faces. One day she had to go into the private part of the house to ask Marieannn advice about one of the school books.

She knocked on the kitchen door. There was no reply. Then she heard the laughter of young children. She opened the door and got such a surprise. Marieann was washing the little girl's hair.. The boy was perched up on the table. Obviously he had been washed and scrubbed. He was eating a huge piece of pie. But it was Marieann who was the biggest surprised. She was no longer a mousy woman. She had discarded her usual snood and Serena noticed how lovely her hair was falling in ripples to her shoulders. But it was her whole being that astonished Serena. There was such happiness shining out of her.

She looked up and spotted Serena. A cloud spread over her face.

"Oh Serena were you looking for me? This poor little girl fell and scratched her knee. They were being chased by some of the village children." She drew Serena aside. "They live with their father. Their mother died. The little boy told me and from what I gather from him their father doesn't bother with them. I'm going to talk to the minister when he gets home tonight. He is away up the valley attending to a family who have had a bereavement. I know that the children would love to be at the school with the other children. Do you think you could take them in?"

"Yes of course I could but maybe the minister could get permission from the father. I don't want any bad feelings." Marieann smiled her lovely smile again and Serena wondered again why she ever thought her mousy.

The minister went to see the children's father. He had no objection. He was just a poor wretch mourning the death of his wife who had died in childbirth. He had no interest in the children and the minister thought he had no longer any interest in living. A few weeks later it came as no surprise to anyone that the poor man was found drowned in the river.

The children would have to be taken into a home. No one knew exactly how things happened so fast. Maybe because he was a minister and a friend of Sir John, papers for the adoption were quickly signed and the minister and Marieann became the parents of the little boy and girl, Peter and Susy.

The weeks and months passed quickly. Serena still took the farm produce to the market once a week. Sometimes near the end of the day when she was packing up, some of the village boys would appear. They just stood around waiting for her to go. They were the ones that the school pupils were afraid of. One day she had to go to the school to pick up a book for Sally. She had to go back past her stall. The village boys were there rummaging about picking up discarded cabbage leaves and squashed fruit. She passed by ignoring them Poor poor children. They must be half starved. And the awful thing about it. Their village was surrounded by farms where there was an abundance of food. She spoke to Seth and Beth about it.

"Well." Seth said. "Their parents could get some work if they wanted. They are a feckless lot and some of the older children could get a few hours work."

"But they will turn out like their parents. Some of these boys are older than Jack and he has been taught to do some work." Serena couldn't quite believe that the children preferred to scavenge than to work or even go to school.

She made a point after that of leaving behind decent vegetables and a few loaves of bread. She made her mind up to visit some of the younger children's parents. Surely they could be helped in some way.

She had never been to the poorer part of the village. There was an air of neglect all around. She knocked at the first house. A young woman answered the door. Two or three young children stood behind her. Before Serena could speak the woman told her to clear off.

"I just want to help." Serena said. "Why don't you let the children come to the school?" "Go to your school?" The woman sneered. "With all the posh farmers' kids. No, my children will stick to their own. We can't afford decent clothes to send them to school. Why don't you ask some of your farmer friends to give our men folk some work. Oh I know we are put down as a lazy thieving lot. Maybe one or two are but why should we all suffer."

Serena turned. The woman had given her a lot to think about. She went to visit Sir John to get advice. They sat for a long time trying to think of a solution that would help the children.

"Well as you know Serena there a lot of times in the year when most of the farmers round about need extra help. I'll go to the village to have a meeting with some of the men folk to see how many are willing to work. I know that a few of them are scroungers and poachers. I can forget about them."

And Sir John organised the meeting between the men and the

farmers with the result that the men were offered work at the busiest times. They were given a promise in writing by Sir John.

Serena, reading the letter that each had received, was puzzled by one of the lines in which he said that the promise to the men had to hold good even if he decided to sell the estate.

The next term at the school saw ten new pupils, shabby clothes but clean and pressed. I will have to have help if this continues she laughed to herself. Everything was just so wonderful.

Serena was correct in thinking that she would need some help in teaching the children. Their ages were so varied. She spoke of it to Marieann. She was surprised when she offered to help. "I could teach the younger children." She said. "After all I have got two of them already." She was talking about the young boy and girl she had recently adopted, Susy and Peter. Serena was delighted. It took such a lot of weight off her shoulders.

She still kept busy at the farm. It was her way of repaying Seth and Beth for all their kindness to her. She fitted in with all the villagers and was invited to all the functions that took place in the village. It was nearly a year since she stumbled from the moor into this happy life she now lived. She was still barely twenty but sometimes she felt so much older. So many things had happened to her since she left the little house on the beach. She still thought a lot about her father. What had happened in his past to make him travel the country with the responsibility of a three year old child. He had been a wonderful father to her. It was because of all his teaching that she was able to take on the work of teaching the village children. Then on the thoughts of her father came the memory of James. Dear kind James. She would never forget him or her first kiss so shyly given from him.

She was busy on the usual Saturday morning setting up the stall in the village with the farm produce. Her thoughts were far away. She was thinking about the new recruits to the school. The change that had come over them since their fathers had found work helping out on the farms. It was all thanks to Sir John and she supposed she had been a bit of help as well.

She reached into the cart to get the urn of milk. It slipped from her hands. The contents covered a man who was standing nearby. "You stupid ignorant peasant." He roared. "I could get you horse whipped for this." She tried to wipe the milk from him and to apologise but he wasn't having it. She lifted her head to look up at him. He was a big man. Black hair with a short black beard. Black eyes that were flashing with temper. He looked foreign. Another man came to join him. He was much smaller and everything about him was pale. Pale hair, pale skin and Serena thought he had the sly look of a weasel. He seemed to be the big man's servant.

A few of the villagers had gathered round when they heard the commotion. One of them shouted at the strangers. "Here don't talk like to the lass. It was an accident. You better be on your way." The big man snarled at him. "Ignorant people."

Serena was upset for the rest of the day. Never in her life, not even in prison, had she been spoken to like that. I hope they never come back to the village. Nobody knew them. They must have just been passing through.

When she got back to the farm she noticed Sir John's carriage. She was always pleased to see him. He was such a wise old man. They were all seated as usual round the kitchen table but there were no smiles on any of their faces.

"Come and sit down." Seth said. "Sir John has come to tell us something.

Sir John started to tell Serena. "I have already told Seth and Beth and I would like you to hear it Serena. You have been such an asset to the village. As you know I am feeling the responsibility of this large estate getting too much for me and I decided to sell. I was in Bridgetown today getting it all finalised. I haven't met the man who bought it. It has all been done through my solicitors but they do inform me that he is young with a young family and that's just what the estate needs. I will be leaving in a few days. I am going to live with my family in Italy." He smiled. "I need the sunshine in my old bones and I am happy that I'm leaving the estate in good hands."

"You have run your farm well Seth. A few of the other farmers have not been doing so well. You have been prepared to try out some of the new ideas to get bigger crops. Maybe next year they will follow your lead."

After Sir John left things carried on as normal. The school had settled into a routine and because the village men were getting a few hours work on the farms there was less poverty in the village. Everyone was waiting to see what the new landlord was like. Some of the farmers were a bit apprehensive. They did not like change.

Serena came home from school after a tiring day. It had taken her ages to convince some school inspectors that the manse was quite suitable to teach the children in. "Would you have preferred the children to have no learning?" She had demanded of one pompous man. Eventually they agreed that the school should remain.

When she entered the house Seth and sally met her with worried faces.

"We have had a bit of bad news Serena." Seth said. "The new landlord has arrived. He visited two of our neighbours. They told me that he was quite unpleasant to them because of the poor yields from their crops. He had hinted that he might have to revoke their tenancies."

One Sunday afternoon the family were all relaxing. It was the only day when they made time if the only work done was to look after the animals. Serena was sitting at the parlour table giving Sally advice about her school work. They all looked up at the sound of a coach pulling up in the yard. Then someone was knocking at the door using it sounded like a riding crop. When Seth, looking worried, answered the door, a loud voice was heard. "This is Rose Dean farm I believe?" "Yes." Seth answered. "And who are you?" Another man's voice answered him. "He is my factor Mullin. And I am your new estate owner Sir Philip Woodstock." Seth ushered them in.

Serena gasped. She was looking at the two awful men from the market. The one she had drenched in milk. She tried to keep her face turned away but when Seth introduced them all she had to look up at the cruel face of Sir Philip Woodstock. He glared at her but said nothing. He spoke to Seth for a few minutes then he turned to Sally. "Where do you work?" Sally all confused didn't answer. "I'm looking for someone to help out at Moorland To work in the house. Beth butted in. "Our daughter is only eleven. She is learning at school and she helps out here with the farm work." "Well think about it." He said. "Sometimes things get difficult and we all have to work." After another minute he was gone. Seth and Beth looked at each other. Was there a threat in his voice?

From that day things never seemed to be the same. It was as if a dark cloud hung over everyone. Serena would sometimes meet them in the village but they would only glare at her never speaking.

It didn't take long before their presence was felt. Two of the smaller farms he would not renew their tenancy. They were turned out and became part of the homeless. Neighbours tried to help but everyone was afraid for their own livelihood and families. If only Sir John had known the awful misery his going had caused. Why had he been so trusting about who would take over the estate?

"Do you think I will have to go to work for him?" Sally kept asking. "What if I don't go and he gets cross with dad. He could take the farm away."

This made Serena think her being at the farm could cause this dear family a lot of trouble. It was obvious that Sir Philip Woodstock would find a way to get back at her not only because of the milk incident but because the locals had defended her.

An air of tension hung about the village. Sir Philip Woodstock just seemed to ride slipshod over some of the agreements that Sir John had made including the written agreement giving some of the village men work. In fact he seemed to take pleasure in telling them to go back home when they turned up for work. Serena felt that she was to blame for this unhappiness but not one of the villagers blamed her, and told her as much, that if there was any more trouble from Sir Philip Woodstock towards her they would defend her again.

One day he marched into the school room when Serena was in the middle of a lesson. He just stood looking around at the children. Two of the older boys ignored him. They carried on practising their writing. It was two of the boys that Serena had rescued by finding a way to get their fathers' some work. Their silence seemed to infuriate him. He marched over to them and banged his riding crop at their desk. "You are both too old to be in school. I have got work for you at Moorlands."

Serena felt her temper rising just as it had done in the prison when she had attacked Isa Jones. She stood in front of Sir Philip and shouted at him. "How dare you come into the school and talk to my pupils like that." "They certainly will not go to work at Moorlands when it is school time. After school it will be up to their parents to decide, not you with your bullying ways."

He lifted the riding crop and for a moment Serena thought he would hit her. His face almost purple with rage, he pulled himself together and marched out to the door. He turned and almost spat at her. "You will get sorted out with your high and mighty ways. Have no doubt about that. Who are you anyway. What brought you to this village?"

That night Serena tossed and turned. She couldn't sleep. What if he found out that she had been in prison for stealing. What would the village people think of her. And the minister. He would be horrified that a thief was teaching his village children. What kind of example was she giving and whatever Sir Philip did find out he would make it as black as possible.

The dawn was breaking when she finally made her decision and that night after school she told the family that she would like to talk to them and they all gathered round the kitchen table. They all looked so worried. Even little Grace, sensing that something was wrong, climbed onto her father's knee, sitting quietly for once.

Serena started to speak. "You know what happened at the school yesterday?" Seth nodded. "Yes Jack and Sally talked about it." He shook his head. "What sort of man is he?" "Well he is the reason that I want to talk to you all. He threatened to find out about me and where I came from. So I want to tell you all my story."

She spoke from the beginning of her first memory with her father right up to the time when they had taken her in half dead from the moor. When she spoke of her time in the prison Beth's tears ran down her cheeks. "So you see." Serena said. "I have to leave." "But you can't." Sally and Jack said together. "We need you at the school." "I'm sorry but Marieann is a good teacher and you Sally will be able to help with the young ones."

Seth had a worried look on his face. "When are you thinking of going Serena? Maybe you should take more time to think about it. Wait at least till the Spring. It's almost a year to the day since you arrived. And in fact the snow isn't far off. I can sense it in the air. But at least you won't be wandering on the moors. We will take you to wherever you want to go."

Chapter 15

Serena shook her head. "No Seth. When I go it must be alone. I don't want Sir Philip to take his spite out on you and try to get you out of the farm." Seth started to disagree with her. "He can't put us out. We still have many years lease left." "No Seth. He is the man with all the money. He would find a way to do it."

No more was said. "We will talk about it later." Seth said. "Maybe things won't look so bad in a few days." Serena wished them all goodnight and made her way to her little room that she had grown to love. She laid a plaid on the floor and started to place her few possessions on to it. She dressed in her warmest clothes and sat writing a note to the family that she had grown to love dearly. She waited till all were asleep then, tying the ends of the plaid together, she slung it over her back and made her way from the farm. Only the dog barking was her farewell.

She walked briskly. She had to get as far as possible from the farm. She also had to keep away from the road. She knew her way for a few miles but later she would have to travel in daylight. The moor was too dangerous a place in the dark.

How could this be happening to her, Running away from something. First of all from Isa Jones and Crawford. Then running away as far as possible from the prison.

She had been so happy with the family at the farm and here she was running away again. All because of that hateful Sir Philip. Why was he so spiteful to her? Then she thought about something Beth had said. "You are young and beautiful Serena. Sir Philip saw in your eyes that you despised him. He would have loved it if you had wanted to please him. After all he was Sir Philip. A wealthy estate owner." "But Beth he is married with children." She remembered saying. "That wouldn't have meant anything." Beth had said. "And because he knew that you were out of his reach, like a spoiled nasty child, what he couldn't have he would destroy."

She trudged along day after day getting more and more weary. She had left the moor behind and decided that she would rest in the next village. A white hoar frost covered the ground and she knew that if she didn't get shelter soon she would perish with the cold.

She rounded a corner of a rough track that she had been following. She got the smell of wood smoke but she couldn't see where it was coming from. She looked around and saw the entrance to a cave. A fire was burning inside.

"Don't just stand there." A woman's voice said. "Come inside and get warm." When she entered she couldn't believe it. It was like a large room. All sorts of bits and pieces that could be had in any cottage. A makeshift bed had brightly coloured covers. Some dishes in a recess shelf along with storage jars. Sheepskin rugs covered the floor.

"You are surprised." The woman said. Serena could only nod. To find something like this cave so many miles from anywhere. She turned to look at the woman. Serena thought she couldn't be more than thirty.

"Come now take off your cloak. It's warm enough in here. It's only when the wind blows from the east it blows straight in." From a pot by the fire she handed her a bowl of stew and on a smooth stone she used as a table she cut her a slice of bread. Serena had never tasted anything so delicious. A strange sound came from the outside. Serena jumped to her feet. The women laughed. "That's Sarah." Serena expected to see maybe an old women come inside but she started to laugh when into the cave came a large goat. "She wanders about all day but at this time every night she comes to get milked and fed." "Then she sleeps near the entrance. She isn't allowed right in. For one reason she has a strong goat smell and for another reason she would eat everything in sight including my clothes."

She handed Serena a plaid. "You tuck that round you and lay down by the fire. Tomorrow there will be plenty time to talk." Even as she finished speaking Serena was asleep.

The early morning light shining in the entrance woke her. She sat up in a panic. What was this strange place? "So you are awake." A woman's voice said. Then she remembered. This kind woman came to her rescue saving her from another cold night on the moor.

"How can I thank you for your kindness?" "Will you keep warm by the fire." She handed her a cup of warm milky tea. She threw more wood on the fire. "Now maybe you will tell me your name. That's all. I don't want to find out anything more about your life. I am Marion King. You are welcome to stay here as long as you want."

"I am Serena Church." "Pretty name." The woman replied. "Now I will have to leave you. I have got to get to the wood to collect more firewood. It's about a mile from here. "Oh please can I come with you to help? I am really very strong." "Well you don't look very strong but come along. I have to get a good supply of firewood before the snow comes. Last year the snow was so heavy I was blocked in."

Serena looked at this woman who was quite prepared to be isolated in her cave. She was, Serena guessed, about thirty years old. Really quite handsome rather than pretty with her strong features. But when she smiled her blue eyes twinkled and one wanted to smile back at her.

They backed up the fire before leaving. Serena stepped outside. She held her breath. It was so beautiful. The early morning sun cast a warm glow over the cliffs and rocks round the cave. She hadn't realised that she had climbed so high in the dark the night before.

Marion pulled a sort of go-cart from behind the rocks. "This is my great helper. I don't know how I would have managed without it. I use it to carry bags of meal and flour from the mill. The village of Darwood is about three miles from the valley floor. I don't go near the village. The mill is as far as I go. It's on the outskirts. Come now. We better get moving. The wood is quite a bit away. We will load the go-cart and go back for a second load."

Serena was exhausted. Marion seemed to have endless energy. In no time most of the wood was stacked at the back of the cave. The rest in big piles near the cave door. "Tomorrow we will do the same and that should keep us going as long as the snow will last." Without halting she had a pot of stew simmering by the fire. Serena guessed it was rabbit. "Now I must attend to Sarah. She will need to be milked and fed.

Sarah had followed them back and forward all day. Sometimes racing ahead. Standing up on the highest rocks. Just showing off Marion said.

They were both ready for bed after supper. Once again Serena slept sound. When she awoke it was a stillness she first noticed. She crawled to the cave entrance. During the night it had snowed quite heavily. There was a strange peace around.

I could stay here forever. Serena thought. Sarah came up to her from where she had been sheltering. Serena thought she just came to say good morning. "Not very much to do today." Marion said coming up behind her. "The cave can be tidied." The sheepskins were lifted from the floor and Marion used a heather broom to sweep the floor. "If you are careful Serena you could fetch water from the little stream just round the corner. I am fortunate that it never seems to freeze."

That night for the first time Marion seemed to want to talk. "You must be wondering why I am so odd living alone in a cave miles from the village."

"Of course I am curious." Serena said. "But Marion that is your business and all I know you have been one of the kindest I have met in my strange travels."

"I feel that I must explain to you. My husband and I had not been married for long. We had met before when we were just young. We had a bit of a romance but we were both independent people. Ivan my husband went to sea and I had decided that I wanted to travel abroad. I'm afraid that I never managed to do that. I had to look after elderly parents. I was an only child. Anyway after a few letters we grew apart. Neither of us had married and just a few months ago we met at a village fair. Ivan asked me to marry him. Neither of us had much money and when we saw an advert in a paper for a gamekeeper with a cottage provided we just jumped at the chance. We were interviewed by an estate manager. It turned out that he had been at sea so Ivan and him had a lot in common. So we moved into the cottage and Ivan was happy at his work. We didn't realise the jealousy from some of the village people. Apparently a few of them had been in for the work

Well a lot of untrue stories about Ivan went to the estate manager. One of them was that he was stealing from the estate. Selling game to the butcher in the next village. The manager ignored the stories. Ivan caught some of the villagers poaching. He reported them. After that the whole village was against us. One night two of the villagers out poaching, one of them with a drink in him, tripped. His gun went off. He was wounded in the legs. They both said that it was Ivan who had tried to kill him. Well to cut a long story short Ivan was sent to prison for three years but because there wasn't enough evidence he didn't get charged with attempted murder. I of course had to leave the cottage and the village. It wasn't safe for me there. Ivan and I in our wanderings found this cave. When I managed to talk to him in prison I told him I would wait for him there. I made a few journeys in the middle of the night to the cottage and I brought all the things you see here. I go to the mill to get some meal and flour. The old miller is a good friend. It was him who gave me the cart to carry the bags. I have Ivan's gun. I can shoot so I can pay the miller for maybe a rabbit or two. This bit of ground for about a mile doesn't belong to anyone. Maybe at one time it might have been common grazing so you see I am bothering no one and I will be here when Ivan is free."

Chapter 16

M arion had hardly stopped to draw breath telling her story. It
was as if she needed someone to talk to. Things that she had
bottled up ever since Ivan's arrest and imprisonment.

"I am happy that you could talk to me." Serena said. "Because you
see the same thing happened to me. I was wrongly accused." She then
proceeded to tell Marion her story.

"You poor girl." Marion reached over and gave her a hug. "I think
you are searching for something. You are at the moment someone
without a past. It's unfortunate that your father was unable to talk to
you."

"That's exactly what a dear friend said to me. It seems like a thousand
years ago." "Oh so you did have a friend." Marion said. "Yes his names
was James. I don't suppose I will ever see him again but I can't forget
him." "How old were you then?" Marion asked. "I had just turned
sixteen. So." She said. "It really was first love." A far away look came
into her face. First love is never forgotten.

"We have done enough talking for one night. Let's get some sleep.
An idea is going on in my head. We will talk about it in the morning.
But meantime I want you to know that I am happy to have you stay as
long as you want."

As usual Marion was first up. She had stoked up the fire to a large blaze, a pot of water boiling ready to make tea. They sat at the cave entrance looking down across the valley. It was so perfect. The snow covering the rocks shone like little diamonds in the early morning sun. Later that day when the few chores were done Marion started to question Serena about what she could remember of her journey before arriving at Crawford.

"But why Marion? What good will it do going back in my mind? I do remember being cold and hungry travelling with my father." "But there must have been some things that still stood out in your memories." Marion insisted. "Apart from your memory of you think about three years of age. What I am trying to do Serena is for you to remember your highlights of your journey to enable you to go back along that way. Now think Serena. Go back and maybe at the end of your journey you will have arrived at your home."

"But it's impossible." Serena almost wailed. "We just travelled over hills and dales, by rivers, through forests. I don't think my father was heading anywhere. He was just running away from something and those two men I think were after him."

"So where did you see the two men Serena?" "At the gypsy camp. We were there for quite a while. We hid when the men came into the camp."

"So there was this camp. Can you remember?" "Oh it was just a camp in a wood. I went to the village with one of the women to sell things." "Can you remember the name of the village?" Marion asked. "No I don't remember. Please stop asking all these questions."

"I'm sorry Serena. My thoughts were if you could remember some place names you could travel back. So you won't like what I am going to suggest now. I think you are desperate to find out who you are. You have always wanted that. So the best starting place is Crawford and let your memory guide you from there."

"It's impossible. I can't go back there. Don't you understand that's where my trouble started. And besides it would take me at least a year to get there."

Marion still insisted. "You could arrive in Crawford at night and leave early in the morning following out the way you had arrived."

"I just can't Marion. I don't think I could walk all those miles again from here to Crawford." "Well my dear what about riding those miles?" Serena just looked at her and laughed. "Ride in what?" "Old Sarah there. No, you worked on a farm. You will know about horses." Serena nodded. "Well there are stables on the far side of the village. They have been known to sell some of their horses. I have a bit of money put by from the short while that Ivan worked so I am going to give it to you to buy a horse."

The next morning Serena set off to find the stables. She was still a bit wary of anyone recognising her. Marion had been right. Two horses were up for sale and she did have admiring glances from some of the stable hands. Maybe, she thought, looking good could have an effect on her getting a good bargain. And it turned out to be the case. The owner, after Serena had said she lived in the village, couldn't have been more helpful.

She left the stables riding a strong looking horse. It would have to be strong for the many miles they would have to travel. They rode back to the cave to get prepared for the journey early the next morning. Serena brushed and petted the horse. She called it Snow because of it's colour and because she would always remember the snow round the cave when he came into her possession. It was a tearful farewell from Marion. So many friends she had made in the past year that she had had to say farewell to. She would never forget her stay in the cave. The beauty of that morning with the snow covering the ground. She had never been taught anything much about religion but that morning she felt close to God.

She was travelling further and further from the sea, the whispering sea, but she was also travelling towards her roots for good or bad to find out what her father had been running from. When Crawford came into sight she felt a pang of sadness. She longed to see Marcus and to visit the beach where she had been so happy with her father and James in the little house. She wondered if she would ever see James again. She put her hand up to her cheek. She could still feel James' kiss, so gentle, so kind. Even although she knew she was taking a chance she had to follow the road. they had used to come into Crawford so many years ago.

Now and again she would come across some landmark that she remembered from the first journey. Then her joy knowing that she was on the right road when she came on the sight of the gypsy camp. It was deserted but she still felt safe there among the trees so she decided to spend the night there.

Early the next morning she couldn't wait to be on her way. What a difference from the first journey with her father, trudging along with the old pram. Dear Marion. Thank you for your help and friendship.

She rode on and on, getting more excited. She came to the farm that they had spent. Oh happy days. Then day after day there were no memories. Nothing to remind her that they had passed that way. Then she cheered up. Of course she would have been too young to remember. It meant that she must be nearing the end of her journey. What would she find. Would it have been better not to know.

All the harshness of the countryside had made way for long expanses of fertile valleys. Animals were grazing the new grass.

She realised that she must look dirty and unkempt so when she came to a wayside inn she decided to spend the night there. Hot water was brought to her room and for the first time in weeks she bathed and washed her hair. The next morning she gathered information about the next part of her journey. A village was about five miles away. Church Town it was called. Serena thought it was a good omen, not unlike her own name of Church.

To travel five miles was nothing for Snow, her sturdy horse.

They entered the village in late afternoon. It was a pretty well cared for village. The church pride of place in the centre.

Chapter 17

She rode through the centre and was surprised to see a small school. Very few villages could boast having one. Education was not important for the working classes or so they thought. The estate owners preferred the children to work for them. Why bother educating them. She was deep in thought and didn't realise that she had left the village and was now riding up a wide drive. I better get back. This seems to be private. She went to turn round then she gasped with astonishment. Towards the end of the drive on raised ground stood the house that her father had painted. Shannon House. Every detail was there. The huge pillars. The verandas. The terraces sloping down to what would be the rose garden. The fountains were spraying into a large pool covered in the water lily leaves but she was sure that when the summer came it would be covered in white and pink water lilies just like the picture her father had painted.

She couldn't control her excitement. Her father must have known the house. He must have lived in the village and it could have been from this village that he had rode away with her. What had he been escaping from? Then the next thought. This is the end of my journey. I can feel it.

She rode back to the village. I've got to find somewhere to stay and find some work. Someone is bound to remember my father. But

I will have to be careful about the questions to ask. She rode back to the inn. She had enough money to stay there for a day or two and to stable Snow.

Jessie the innkeeper's wife was very sympathetic when Serena asked if there was any work in the village. "No I'm afraid not my dear. Besides ourselves there is only a small guest house and the village shop that provide work for the villagers. Maybe you could try some of the farms. They may take someone on for the spring planting."

"That's a good idea Jessie. I'll try that. I have worked on a farm." "Now where would that be? Asked Jessie, her head to one side like an inquisitive blackbird. Serena managed to sidestep the question by asking about the big Mansion House. That got her going. "Now Jack my man and I only came here to run this inn a year back. It belongs to the big house estate along with the whole village. Nobody about here talks much about the owners. I think myself that there is a bit of a mystery about the place but they seem to be good to all those who work for them."

"I believe that all their money was made by one of the ancestors in a diamond mine in Africa. Some say that they went from Ireland to Africa. That is why it is called Shannon House after an Irish river. For the same reason that this village is called Church Town after the generations of the name of Church at the Mansion House. They have an overseer who takes care of everything. Some say that the lady of the House is never seen but the staff are a close mouthed lot. After all they would have too much to loose if they were caught gossiping. Not only would it be their work but their homes as well. It's just as well you don't work there Serena thought to herself.

Just then Jack came in. He glared at his wife. "I hope you aren't talking about things that don't concern you. That tongue of yours could get us into trouble." "Now Jack how could I gossip about something I don't know." She turned to Serena. "He worries because this inn is part of the estate."

Poor Jack Serena thought. Jessie would never be able to keep quiet about anything. But she was grateful to her for the information she had given her. Wasn't it strange that at the Mansion they should have the same name as her. But then she realised that it was quite common for workers on an estate to take the name of the owners because, as she found out through Jessie, the Churches had been there for many generations.

The next day she left the inn early. She rode for miles knowing in her heart that this was her father's home. It gave her comfort just being there. Maybe had worked on one of the farms.

Deep in thought she rode back into the village. A shout brought her to her senses. She had almost knocked down a man stepping out from the village shop. She jumped down from Snow. "I am so terribly sorry." "No harm done." The man said. He was a tall good looking man, an air of authority about him. Maybe a schoolteacher. "I'm just as much to blame as you." He said. "I too was day dreaming." He had a lovely smile.

"I hope it was something nice that you were dreaming about." He said. "Well not really. I'm trying to find some work but so far there seems to be nothing." "What kind of work?" He was looking at her underneath her riding hat. He could see the delicate features that went with her refined accent. "I don't suppose you would be interested in gardening?"

"Why yes. I love gardening." "Well well, we are well met. I am looking for a gardener to help out one of the old men. The work is getting too much for him. He has been in the garden for many years." "I don't want to let him go. That's what I was doing in the shop. Putting up a notice for a gardener to help him. I have another five gardeners working."

"Gosh." Serena said. "It must be a big garden. More like a park." "Well." The man smiled. "You could maybe call it that. It's at Shannon House. I'm Mark Steven. I'm the overseer of the estate."

Serena was overjoyed to work in the garden that her father had painted. Maybe he too had worked in the garden.

"So you will take the job?" He asked. "Yes of course I would love to." "Well." He continued. "There is accommodation for the staff. I think you would be happy there. It is quite comfortable. And what is your name horse woman? "Oh." She said. "Sorry. I'm Serena Church." "Well isn't that strange. Another Church."

Serena had the feeling that he didn't believe that was her name. That for reasons of her own she just made it up. But nothing mattered. She had work and she had somewhere to live and maybe she might discover the mystery of what her father was running away from.

She rode up to Shannon House early the next morning. As she came in sight of it it seemed even more beautiful the second time. The early morning sun picked out all the turrets making them look golden. Why it's like something out of a fairy tale castle.

Away to the left of the garden partly hidden was a row of whitewashed cottages. She guessed that it must be for the workers. She made her way to them and was met by an old man who was just leaving one of them. She felt like laughing. He looked just like one of the dwarfs from a fairy tale and he seemed to be in keeping with the magic of Shannon House. He was such a happy looking old man with his rosy cheeks and white hair and even the uniform. He was wearing trousers and a tunic of leaf green fitted the picture perfectly. He smiled at Serena. "I have been expecting you my dear." Then he gave her a puzzled look. "Haven't we met before?" He answered himself. "Forgive me my dear. I do go rambling on. The old memory plays tricks. Come inside." He led her into one of the cottages. On the door was a little plaque stating that it was Rose Cottage. "All the cottages have flower names. So much nicer than numbers." The old man explained. "Now my cottage is the next one to you. It's called Hollyhock. Quite fitting for me because it's one of the oldest flowers. I believe your name is Serena. Very pretty again." He gave her an odd look. "I'm called Digger for obvious reasons. When you are ready come and join me at the veg garden." He gave her such a lovely smile. Serena felt that she could hug him.

The inside of the little cottage was neat and compact. A little room that held a bed enclosed in drapes. The room was used for a bedroom and living room. Through a door was a little closet used for toilet and washing. A good pile of logs was stacked beside the open fire which she would probably have to light each evening when she got home from work. Everything was spick and span. The table had been scrubbed so many times the wood was almost white. The same with the wooden floor. Oh I'm going to be so happy here. Serena hugged herself. I'm so glad. I feel that father is looking after me.

She washed quickly and for the first time she saw a uniform lying on the bed. It was similar to Digger's but she had a home spun skirt in leaf green. They fitted her perfectly. How strange. Then she realised that all the gardeners wore this uniform. It would have been easy to guess the size of a young woman when the overseer explained to the woman in charge of the uniforms inside and outside the house. She made her way to the vegetable garden. Digger was already busy there. He smiled at Serena. "You look just like a green goddess coming out of the wood." Serena laughed. "Now let us start preparing the ground for early potatoes." Digger handed her a spade. And so her first day at Shannon House began.

Chapter 18

M ark Steven the overseer came to see how she was getting on. In among all the other green uniforms her beauty stood out. A bit of a mystery about that young lady he thought to himself. But she is a plucky one keeping up with the rest of the workers.

When lunchtime came all the outside staff met in one of the outside buildings. A long table covered the floor from end to end. Enough room for about twenty people. It was done up like a proper canteen. Three of the village women served up from large pots. A meat course and a pudding was served every lunchtime. The women walked about the garden at the afternoon break serving tea and a bun, the large urn pulled along on a trolley. No wonder the staff at Shannon House stayed for their lifetime. At the end of the day Serena made her way back to the little Rose Cottage. She was tired but happy. Everyone had been so kind to her. Digger treated her like a daughter. Throughout the day he gave her helpful tips on plants.

She knelt down to light the fire and suddenly from nowhere the tears came. It was the memory of lighting the fire at the beach house and of losing to dear people her father and James who was as good as dead to her.

Day followed day. She watched the garden bursting into bloom. It was exactly as her father had painted it. The rose garden with it's hundreds of blooms. All that was missing was the figure of a woman among them.

Then one Sunday afternoon everything was quiet about the garden. She decided to go exploring. She passed the rose garden then she stopped. A woman was there picking the roses. She was dressed completely in black. A black veil covered her from the top of her head to her chest.

It was impossible to guess her age. Her father had painted a beautiful young woman but of course that had been many years ago. After all it was only a painting. Her father could have just used the woman for effect. She must have made a noise. The woman looked at her directly then picking up her basket of roses she walked quickly away out of sight behind one of the hedges.

How strange Serena thought. Maybe it was someone stealing the roses. She mentioned it to Digger when they all met for tea. He looked quite taken aback for a moment. "Oh she could be one of the women from the village. They are allowed to gather flowers for the church." It was left at that but Serena wasn't completely satisfied. Why had she left in such a hurry without speaking.

One day when they were sitting having their lunch she asked Digger what the big house was like inside. "Oh well I've only seen the kitchen and the ballroom. Once a year a big ball is given. When I was younger I was sometimes asked to help out at waiting. It was all so grand. The ballroom is all red and silver. It is a long room. Four crystal chandeliers make it as bright as day. On a warm night the doors are opened out to the garden. The guests wander outside with their drinks, the smell of the roses hedy, competing with the ladies' perfumes."

"It sounds wonderful. Do you think there will be a ball this year?" "Yes but my Lady doesn't attend since she lost her husband."

Serena was wanting Digger to go on talking. Maybe her father would have been one of the ones asked to help at the ball. But then she thought what if he had to leave the village in disgrace. Digger wasn't wanting to do any more talking. He looked a bit uncomfortable.

"I'm just an old man rambling on." Serena couldn't help asking another question. "What does my Lady look like?" Digger turned an angry face to her. "She is beautiful inside and out. Now please stop being so inquisitive and get some work done. We don't gossip here." Serena felt well and truly put in her place. Thank goodness she hadn't asked if he knew her father.

Digger, walking with her to work the next morning, couldn't control his excitement.

"Guess what Serena. The grand ball is taking place in two weeks. The invitations have already been sent out." From then on the work in the gardens intensified. Serena thought that everything was already perfect but not so Digger. Even with his failing sight he would spot one of the lawn edges out of a straight line.

The rose garden got the special attention. Digger told her that her Ladyship would decide the day before the ball the colour of the roses she wanted on the tables dotted round the room.

The water lily pond was cleaned and all the dead lily leaves removed. It was a beautiful sight with all the pink and white lilies in full bloom. It took five men to clean it.

"What a wonderful month to have a ball here," she said to Digger. "It has always got to be the month of June. It is the anniversary of the time she lost her husband." Serena said nothing though once again she wanted to ask what had happened to him.

The overseer had a busy time. He knew that many of the guests would be staying for a few days would love to wander round the huge estate visiting even some of the farms which were miles away.

"You are wanted to bring a basket of eggs up to the big house," Digger told her about two days before the ball. "Straight there and back. No hanging about. Go straight to the kitchen."

Serena collected the huge basket of eggs from the poultry farm. She was all excited. At last she was going into the house even although it was only to the kitchen. She walked round to the back and close to the house she realised how huge it was. It took her some time to find the door into the kitchen. So many different rooms. One room she passed a man was busy polishing silver. The whole room was packed with it. Then there were rooms with all sorts of riding clothes and boots. There again a man busy polishing. She looked into she supposed was a pantry full of cake stands and a huge assortment of plates and china. Next to it a scullery with it's huge sinks for washing pots and pans. Gosh, she thought. Will I ever find the kitchen. Just then a bell started to ring. She looked up along the corridor. Up in the wall was a long line of bells. A man came to look up. Serena had never seen anyone like it. He had a white wig tied at the back with a green ribbon. He wore pantaloon trousers that came to his knee tied with a buckle. A short jacket with a white frilled blouse. On his feet black shoes. Buckled white stockings reached to his knees tucked into his pantaloons.

His clothes were the same green as all the workers but his was beautiful velvet. He reached up and stopped the bell. He didn't even look at Serena standing there. At last she found the kitchen. It was a huge room. There were maybe about ten women there. They all wore green but it was mostly covered with large crisp white aprons. As she stood there the man from the hall shouted in the door. "That was my Lady on the bell. She wants white roses on the ballroom tables." Serena handed over the basket quickly. Digger would be wondering what had happened to her. She couldn't wait to tell him about the strange man. Serena thought he would never stop laughing when she told him.

"That was one of the footmen. The are about ten of them. Yes they do look a bit funny I suppose but that is tradition that they dress like that. It goes back hundreds of years. As for the colour green on all the workers. That goes back many years. Haven't you thought the name of the house, Shannon and the colour green all linked with Ireland." "Oh but of course. How stupid of me." But she was glad that Digger was back to his old self again. The thought of the grand ball seemed to take years off him. I suppose over twenty years ago he would have been in the thick of all the celebrations.

All the coming and going to the big house. Butchers and bakers to the kitchen to be given their orders. The lady in charge of the bedchambers making sure that everything was perfect for the guests. Then a group of floral designers working throughout the day to arrange the flowers in all the rooms as well as the ballroom. The excitement of it all reached even to the outlying parts of the estate. The day before the ball the coaches started to arrive. First to arrive was a gentleman on his own.

Serena and Digger from a vantage point in the garden watched all the coming and going. "That gentleman," Digger informed her, "is a cousin of Lord Church. He will be the next heir. He is married with two daughters. He is a kind gentleman but his family. Digger made a grimace." Serena was surprised. It was so unlike him. Now why? "Were his wife and daughters not with him," she asked. "Oh they will arrive in another coach shortly. They like to make sure that everything is ready for their arrival. In other words they like the servants to be lined up for their arrival." While Digger was speaking another coach arrived. It was the wife and two daughters. The girls looked to be about the same age. Maybe eighteen and twenty. Both fair haired and quite tall. But there was little to see of their faces. They seemed to be covered in satin cloaks with large stand up collars. Almost identical. One in blue and one in pink.

The mother was very tall. She wore a lot of jewellery that sparkled when the sun caught it. Serena got the impression of a long face. Her voice strident reached to the watchers. "Do be careful with that case, stupid man." The poor footman was in trouble.

Then all the coaches started to arrive. The ladies all in their silks and satins. They milled about shaking hands. Obviously they all seemed to know each other. Some of them wandered into the garden. "Just to stretch my legs darling," one of them was saying. "I can't wait to see the rose garden again."

Serena and Digger turned to make a hasty retreat. Another coach had arrived. Serena stopped to have a quick look. A young lady of her own age stepped out. She was lovely. Fair hair piled high on her head fastened with some jewel. She was small and dainty dressed in palest pink. Her shoes matched her dress. The gentleman followed her out of the coach. Serena gasped. She blinked. Surely it's just because I had just been thinking about him. It can't be. Digger turned round. "Serena." He caught her before she collapsed onto the ground. "Whatever is the matter with you child?"

"The man that just came out of that coach was the dearest friend of my life. His name is James Lorrimar." Digger looked at her and thought to himself. I think she thought of him as more than a friend.

He helped her home holding onto her. He was quite shocked at the state she was in. It wasn't the same Serena that had worked alongside him. He sat her down and busied himself getting the fire going. After a while she started to compose herself.

"I'm so sorry Digger to have made such a fuss and nuisance. I'll be all right now." Digger turned from tending the fire. He looked at her. Some of the tears were still on her cheeks. She reminded him of someone else that he had had to comfort many years before. He patted her hand. "Now Serena don't you think it would help if you told me your whole story." Serena looked at him. This dear old man who had been so kind to her.

"Yes Digger. Maybe it would help you to understand why I got so upset." She commenced to tell her story. Once or twice Digger got up to tend the fire. It was to hide the look of excitement on his face as Serena's story unfolded.

When she finished Digger wrapped a blanket round her because of the shivering she was doing. It was as though she was suffering from shock. Her eyes cleared. It was as if a weight had been lifted from her. Digger tip toed out. He was surprised that the sun was still shining brightly and all the laughter was still coming from the big house, all the guests still milling about.

It was well into the night when Digger made his way up to Shannon House. He entered in the back door. Nobody challenged him. The footmen and butlers were all busy attending to all the guests in the ballroom. He made his way up corridor after corridor till he came to the main stairway. It rose from the front hall. The music was louder and when two of the guests opened one of the doors he could see into the ballroom. He caught a glimpse of the dancers.

He made his way up the stairs. It was carpeted in a thick luxurious wine colour. The ornate banisters beautifully carved with gold insets. He moved down another long corridor. It was silent. Not a sound reached it from the ballroom. He knocked loudly on a thickly engraved door which had the Church coat of arms. After a short interval it was opened by a woman dressed entirely in black. She greeted Digger warmly. She had a beautiful soft voice with just a slight trace of a foreign accent. She led him into a large sitting room. It seemed to be full of sunshine. The colours of the furniture were covered in yellow and gold brocade matched the thick honey covers carpet and curtains. White French furniture dotted about the room which led out to a balcony opening out to a view of the rose garden. She motioned Digger to one of the couches. "Now my dear friend what brings you to see me?"

Digger looked at her. He thought she was even more beautiful now than when she first came to Shannon House, a frightened young girl from another country. Digger remembered their first meeting. He was a young waiter afraid that he might do something wrong when one of his duties was to serve her ladyship afternoon tea in this very room. The first time he entered she couldn't have heard his timid knock. She was on her knees beside the fire surrounded by piles of ledgers. She was crying. "How can I do this?" There were ledgers for the kitchen, the pantry, the bedrooms and for all the different departments. She looked up and saw him standing watching. He remembered how embarrassed she was. And because he was so young he had had the nerve to put out his hand and pull her to her feet and give her advice. "Now my Lady why don't you gather up all these ledgers and give them to the administrator of the house." She had looked at him. "Could I really do that?" "But of course you could my Lady," he had told her. "Why don't you just ring for one of the footmen and tell him to give them to the administrator. I'm quite sure you were just supposed to give them a quick glance. You were I'm sure just giving you your place as the head of the running of the house."

She had put her hand out to the cord to summon the footman then she had withdrawn it. "Can I really do this," she had asked. He remembered placing his hand over hers and giving the cord a good pull. He made himself scarce at the other end of the room and was so happy for her when she gave the order. And the footman gathered up the ledgers and said. "Certainly my Lady. I will take them to the administrator's office." She almost danced about the room after that and a bond was made between them and he was always there to help her.

He looked again at the beautiful woman beside him. The beautiful white skin, blue eyes which were such a contrast to the jet black hair. She turned to smile at him and even although throughout the years he had never got used to the terrible scar that turned her smile into a terrible grimace. His heart ached for her. "Come now Digger," she was saying. "When you entered this room I felt that there was something important you wanted to talk about. You seem so excited."

"Oh my Lady I think there is and while I look at you I am more convinced of it."

"Digger please stop rambling on," she said. "I want you to sit down my Lady to prepare for a shock. I think I have found your daughter."

She fumbled for a chair. It was as if all the power went from her legs. She said nothing. Just looked at him with such a pitiful look like a small hurt child. After a while she whispered. "Digger please, please repeat what you just said."

Digger sat down and repeated word for word what Serena had told him about her life. When he came to the part about Serena's father dying she jumped and started walking about the room wringing her hands. "Oh what a sad waste of both our lives. My David. My darling husband. If only he understood how much I loved him. He was my life. That night all those years ago when he left and done this to me." She put her hand up to the scar on her cheek. "It was all a terrible misunderstanding. It all happened out of jealousy. You will remember Digger what he was like. He was so possessive. I was just a seventeen year old girl with very strict French parents. We lived in a small village.

My family had for generations been wine growers. Anyway I was sent to Paris to live with an English family. I wanted to study art. Anyway to cut such a long story short a cousin of my father came to look me up to see if I was getting on alright with my studies. I think it was to see if I was behaving. Anyway Simon was just a few years older than me and he was great fun. He was like a breath of fresh air."

The English family were stricter than my parents. He took me to a skating rink one evening. I wasn't very good. I kept on falling. Twice I just about knocked a tall good looking Englishman off his feet. We laughed and cousin Simon of course started to talk to him. We ended up all sitting drinking chocolate.

Anyway Simon went back home and I continued to meet the tall Englishman David Church. We fell in love. I took him home to meet my parents and they seemed to approve. Dad did not mention that one day he would be a Lord. About two years after our first meeting we were married. I never met David's mother. She had been dead for some years. His father was in ill health. He died a year after we were married so my David became Lord David Church and I became mistress in this mansion. I was very lonely. David couldn't get me interested in all the hunting and shooting. The only thing I loved was working in the garden. David would sometimes be away for days at a time. The night of the ball he had been away shooting in Scotland.

I was thrilled when my cousin Simon arrived. He hadn't seen my lovely little daughter. He made such a fuss of her of course even although she was just a child. I had very little say in her upbringing but Simon was having none of it."

"He defied the nanny and the governors and had her racing about the house shrieking with laughter. He decided to wait for the ball and leave very early at dawn. His servant had both horses packed ready for the journey. It was a wonderful ball. I had had a beautiful yellow dress made. I know that I looked beautiful and I defy any good looking woman not to admit that fact even although it's only to herself and they enjoy the attention they are given.

So it was that night that it all happened. David had not arrived. I was dancing with Simon. I think maybe flirting a little. Then everything seemed to happen. I looked up and saw David standing at the door. His face was white with anger. I saw the gun in his hand. I felt pain and apparently I nearly died. It was weeks afterwards that I came to. I had lost my husband and my child.

Piecing it all together from the witnesses David had thought that the two horses packed for leaving were for Simon and me, that I was leaving him. He thought that he had killed me and that he would hang. That was why he ran, taking the only thing left in his life, the child.

By the time she had finished her story the tears were running down her cheeks and she kept saying, my poor child, that she should have suffered because of her parents mistakes. Digger tried to comfort her. "But you can make it up to her now." She shook her head. "Nothing can make up for all these wasted years. Imagine it Digger. A child of mine. No shoes on her poor little feet."

Eventually she slept and Digger hurried out. It was almost dawn. He felt drained. All he wanted was to get home to his own little place and sleep. In the morning after a few hours sleep he felt able to talk to Serena. She met him at the door before he had time to knock. She was dressed in her working clothes. He could tell that she too had had little sleep, her face drawn and pale.

"I don't want you to work this morning Serena. Go inside. I have got something to tell you." Serena listened to what he had to tell her. A look of shock came on her face followed by such happiness. "My mother is in Shannon House?" "No Serena. Your mother owns Shannon House. She is waiting there to welcome you home. We will go there now."

"Oh Digger. Do you think she will love me?" He gave her a quick hug. "Yes my dear. She will love and cherish you."

Digger led her through the house. There was such a change from her first visit. Servants were dashing hither and thither attending to the guests. They got curious looks.

Digger as before knocked on the door. This time a servant opened it. He asked their names shooting them a disdainful look. He looked startled when her Ladyship's voice told him to admit them.

Serena and her mother looked at each other saying nothing. Serena saw a beautiful woman who looked too young to be her mother and Lady Church looked at Serena her daughter. It was like looking at herself when she was just a young girl.

Instantly they moved into each others arms. All the years of separation and heartache forgotten. Digger left them. He felt tears in his own eyes.

It didn't take long for the whole house to hear of the return of the lost daughter. There was great excitement throughout the house, everyone wanting to catch a glimpse of her But for two days they waited in vain. For days boxes started to arrive from all sorts of shops. Two dressmakers were hired.

Among all the excitement Serena sat, a sad look on her face, her mother worried about it. "Some thing is troubling you Serena. Won't you tell me. Are you unhappy living in this house?" Serena hugged her mother. "I have never been happier but all the grandeur would mean nothing without you."

"I'm sorry if I seem sad but I must tell you that the young man who stayed with us at the beach was so kind and gentle. I have hoped to meet him again but it wasn't to be."

"Serena." Mother looked at her. "Do you think that maybe your feelings for this young man was more than friendship?"

"I just know that I have thought about him ever day throughout the years and a few days ago I saw him. He is one of your guests but he was with a lovely young lady. It could be his fiance or his wife." "Well I can soon find that out my darling. What's his name?" Serena told her. "James Lorrimar." She rang a bell and when the footman answered she asked him to bring the book with all the guest names. They sat at the table going through the guest list one by one.

She gave a chuckle when she pointed to the names of the cousin with the wife and two daughters. "We won't be seeing much more of them thank goodness. You turning up put an end to their ambitions of being Lord and lady Church." Then her finger pointed to the name on the book. James Lorrimar and partner Jane King. "Why I know of this," her mother said. She looked at the back of the folder. "Yes here it is." A letter from Nigel King stating that he would be held up for a day and had asked his cousin James Lorrimar to escort his wife who had been so disappointed at not being able to go to the ball with no escort.

Sitting about in the lounges the only topic of conversation was Lady Church's daughter. James Lorrimar, sitting with his cousin Nigel King and his wife Jane, were just as interested. Jane was thrilled. "It's just like a fairy tale," she said.

One of the footmen came into the lounge. He looked around then he made his way over to James Lorrimar and tapped him on the shoulder. "Her Ladyship would like to have a word with you. Will you follow me Sir." James, completely puzzled, followed him up the stairs into a spacious drawing room. A slim woman standing by the fire held out her hand. "Mr Lorrimar. I am Lady Church." He was shocked when she turned and he saw the terrible scar on her face but she still looked beautiful and she reminded him of someone.

"Do sit down James. May I call you that?" He nodded feeling a bit bemused. Do you remember a young girl called Serena Church?" James sat bolt upright. "Yes yes, indeed I do. I searched high and low for her. I visited her old friend Marcus two or three times but she hadn't been in touch with him. I've never stopped thinking about her."

"Did she ever tell you her story?" "Yes," he said "Some bits of it but her father wasn't keen on her talking." "Her father died." "Oh I'm sorry to hear that." Lady Church sat quiet for a while. "What is this about My Lady?"

"I know where Serena is." James jumped to his feet. "Please tell me. It would make me so happy." "She is at the moment in the rose garden. You may go there to find her."

No sooner had she finished speaking when James, after a quick curtsy, made for the door. Lady Church smiled.

James almost ran to the rose garden. He would never ever forget the moment that he saw Serena. She had a basket of roses over her arm. She wore a simple white dress. Her long black hair fell to her waist. He stopped. Then he remembered the picture her father had painted. It looked exactly like what he was seeing now. Aware that someone was watching she lifted her head and looked straight at him then just like the young girl on the beach she ran to him. It was the most natural thing in the world for them to put their arms round each other and find each others lips. There was no need for long explanations. They had after so many years found each other.

James wanted to hear every detail of Serena's life. At times he, like Lady Church, was near to tears. "Please James don't be sad. I met wonderful friends." Serena hugged him. "And after all I met you."

Within weeks arrangements were being made for their wedding. Serena would have liked something quiet but because of her position that was impossible. One thing she insisted on was that all the good people that had been kind to her should be invited.

A coach was sent round with the gilt edged invitations to the mightiest and the poorest. One of the servants couldn't believe it that he had to deliver to a cave high on a hill. Another had to search the streets for a friend called Amy.

They all started to arrive at Shannon House. Serena greeted them all. A special hug for Amy, still a poor half starved girl. The servant searching for her to present her with the invitation almost ran over her as she was getting thrown out of a bakers shop. "You thieving brat," he was shouting. "Don't come back here."

From the moment she got the invitation to the morning of the wedding Amy's mouth never closed. She was going to work here at Shannon House as Serena's maid. She was standing among the guests waiting to go into the church when she overheard a grim faced woman speaking to her husband and daughters. "This could have been yours if that Serena hadn't turned up. Look at some of the guests. Such common people," she sniffed. "If you ask me Serena is just as common." The next moment she felt a push. She fell flat out on the ground. Unfortunately for her one of the coach horses had just emptied its bowel on that very spot. Amy with an innocent look walked on into the church.

The early morning sun turned the sails of the ship sailing round the headland into gold.

It anchored just off shore. A young couple with their arms round each other stood on the prow looking towards the shore and a little ramshackle house. A small dinghy was lowered and the young couple walked towards the little ramshackle house.

They stood not speaking for a while. Then the man said. "I am going to repair it. " "And I am going to help you. It will be our favourite place in the world."

"I love you Serena." "And I love you James."

Serena bent down and removed her shoes. "Come on James." She ran into the sea. "I'll race you to where we first listened to the whispering sea."

THE END.